喚醒你的英文語感！

Get a Feel for English !

Get a Feel for English !

喚醒你的英文語感！

BIZ English

Office English

搞定

辦公室英文

總編審⊙王復國
作　者⊙Brian Foden

Office English

想在職場不敗，英文溝通是必備能力。
從基本應對到辦公室內高頻議題，
擁有本書，輕鬆搞定！

16 個辦公室高頻情境
32 個擬真對話範例
256 個基本應對必通句
128 個化解難題加分句

貝塔語言出版
Beta Multimedia Publishing

附1片實戰MP3

PREFACE

Have you ever heard or seen an English word or phrase, and then thought to yourself, "I know that word! I've seen it before, but ... I just can't remember it!" If you have, it probably means that you don't really "know" that word yet, you've just "encountered" it. It may have been in your short-term memory for a while, but now it's gone.

Most of us, when we encounter a new word or phrase, look the phrase up in a dictionary, and then repeat it to ourselves several times in an attempt to memorize it. This approach is largely ineffective. Language experts say that we need to be exposed to a new word or phrase at least five times—in different contexts—before we will be able to remember it, and before it will go into our long-term memory.

The late Dr. Pimsleur, one of the world's leading experts in applied linguistics, developed a theory to explain this phenomenon, which he called "Graduated Interval Recall." This theory says that target words and phrases need to be introduced at periodic intervals for them to move from short-term into long-term memory. Dr. Pimsleur also advocated mastering the "Core Vocabulary" of any language—those words and phrases that occur most frequently, and which from the foundation of language proficiency.

Beta's Biz English series was designed with Pimsleur's theories about language and memory in mind. In this installment, readers are taught 384 core phrases for office communication. Each phrase is introduced once, along with a sample sentence. Then, many of the phrases are repeated again in the "Show Time" dialogue in each chapter, where readers can see how the phrase is used in larger context.

It's often said that "repetition is the mother of mastery," and there is no area where this is more true than in learning a foreign language. Devote yourself to studying the content in this book, and to listening to the accompanying MP3, and you won't just have encountered the material, you'll have really learned it!

Happy Studying,

Mark Hammond

英文主編序

你有沒有曾經聽到或看到某個英文單字或用語，然後心裡想：「我認識這個單字！我看過，可是……我就是想不起來！」如果你有這種經驗，就表示你還沒真正「認識」這個字，你只是曾經「遇見」它。也許這個字存在你的短期記憶裡有那麼一下子，不過現在卻煙消雲散了。

遇到新的單字或用語時，我們大部分的人會查字典，然後複誦個幾遍試圖背起來，但這種方法的效果十分有限。語言專家指出，我們要在不同語境中接觸到一個字或詞至少五次才能把它們記起來，我們的長期記憶也才能加以儲存。

已故的保羅‧皮姆斯勒博士是全球應用語言學界的翹楚，他發展出一種理論來解釋此現象，他稱之為「漸進式間歇回想」。這種理論認為目標單字或用語必須經過週期性間隔導入，才能從短期記憶化為長期記憶。皮姆斯勒博士也提倡熟悉任一語言裡的「核心字庫」，也就是最常被使用、構成精通該語言基礎的字詞。

貝塔的商用英文書系是依皮姆斯勒博士針對語言和記憶的理論設計而成。在這本書裡，讀者會學到 384 個辦公室溝通所需的核心句型。每種句型會附一個例句呈現，而其中許多句型會在每章「Show Time」對話單元中重複出現，這時候讀者能夠領略如何把這類句型用在更廣的語境中。

常有人說「反覆能造就精通」，這句話用在學習外語上再正確也不過了。希望你能全心吸收本書內容，並認真聆聽搭配的 MP3，你將不只是與教材內容匆匆交會，而是實實在在學會了。

祝各位學習愉快。

Mark Hammons

CONTENTS

第 十四 章　讓上司印象深刻與讚美同事
Impressing the Boss and Complimenting Coworkers

第 十五 章　辦公室八卦 Office Gossip

第 十六 章　談論目標與未來計畫
Talking About Goals and Future Plans

實戰演練 Answer Keys

和同事初次見面與問候
Meeting and Greeting Collegues

Whether you're a new employee or a long-time veteran of a company, meeting someone new in the workplace can be a little uncomfortable if you don't know some important phrases. This chapter will help you easily talk about your job responsibilities, as well as introduce new employees to the other workers.

無論你在公司是新進員工還是資深老鳥，如果對幾個重要的詞語不熟悉的話，在工作場所和人初次見面時便可能會有些不自在。本章將幫助你輕鬆開口談論自己的職責，並將新員工介紹給其他同事認識。

1 Biz 必通句型 Need-to-Know Phrases

 track 02

1.1 介紹新員工 Introducing a New Employee

❶(Person's name), I'd like you to meet (other person's name).

（某人的姓名），我介紹（另一人的姓名）給你認識。

例 Ted, I'd like you to meet Susan.

泰德，我介紹蘇珊給你認識。

❷(New employee's name) is new to the company.

（新員工的姓名）是公司的新進人員。

例 Jennifer, this is Art. Art is new to the company.

珍妮佛，這位是亞特。亞特是公司的新進人員。

❸This/It is (new employee's name)'s first day on the job.

今天是（新員工的姓名）到職的第一天。

例 This is Paul's first day on the job.

今天是保羅到職的第一天。

❹(Person's name) is our (job title).

（姓名）是我們的（職銜）。

例 Fred, this is Tony. Tony is our sales manager.

佛萊德，這位是東尼。東尼是我們的業務經理。

❺ (New employee's name) used to be with (employee's former company).

（新員工的姓名）以前在（員工之前的公司）工作。

例 Frank used to be with Computer Electronics Inc.

法蘭克以前在電腦電子公司工作。

❻ Everyone, I'd like you to welcome (name) to the company.（將某人介紹給一群人認識）

各位，我想請大家歡迎（姓名）加入公司。

例 Everyone, I'd like you to welcome Sandy to the company.

各位，我想請大家歡迎珊蒂加入公司。

❼ Let's welcome (name) to the company.（將某人介紹給一群人認識）

讓我們歡迎（姓名）加入公司。

例 Let's welcome Debbie to the company.

讓我們歡迎黛比加入公司。

❽ I'd like you to all introduce yourselves to (new employee's name).（請同仁主動自我介紹）

我希望大家把自己介紹給（新員工的姓名）認識。

例 Everyone, this is Fiona. I'd like you to all introduce yourself to Fiona sometime today.

各位，這位是費歐娜。我希望大家今天找時間把自己介紹給費歐娜認識。

1.2 談論自己的工作 Talking About Your Job

❶ I'm in (job field or department).
我在（工作領域或部門）。
例 Hi, my name's Tony. I'm in marketing.
嗨，我叫東尼，我在行銷部。

❷ I work in (job field or department).
我在（工作領域或部門）工作。
例 I work in the accounting department.
我在會計部工作。

❸ My duties include (doing sth.).
我的職責包括（做某些事）。
例 My duties include creating advertising and <u>promotional</u> material.
我的職責包括製作廣告和促銷文宣。

❹ I'm responsible for (area or task).
我負責（領域或任務）。
例 I'm responsible for the engineering department.
我負責工程部門。

Word List
promotional [prə`moʃən]] *adj.* 促銷的

❺ I'm in charge of (field).

我負責（領域）。

例 I'm in charge of production.

我負責生產。

❻ My hours are (time period).

我上班的時間是（時段）。

例 My hours are from 8:30 a.m. to 5:30 p.m.

我上班的時間是上午八點半到下午五點半。

❼ I work the day/night/afternoon shift.

我上的是早／晚／午班。

例 I work the night shift.

我上的是晚班。

❽ I've worked for this company for (time).

我已經在這家公司工作（時間）了。

例 Hello, my name's Betty. I've worked for this company for seven years.

你好，我叫貝蒂，我已經在這家公司工作七年了。

ord List

in charge of 照顧（管理，擔任）……

shift [ʃɪft] *n.* 輪班（制）；換班時間；輪換的班

2 實戰會話 Show Time

2.1 到職第一天 The First Day on the Job

 track 03

Today is Darren Jiang's first day on the job at Wang, Hsiao and Tung (WHT), an engineering firm in Taiwan. WHT's <u>personnel</u> manager, Amanda Sharp, is introducing Darren to other members of WHT's staff.

Amanda: Steve Fong, I'd like you to meet Darren Jiang. It's Darren's first day on the job.

Steve: Hi Darren. It's nice to meet you. I'm responsible for WHT's projects in Europe. Good to have you with the company.

Darren: Thanks, Steve. It's great to meet you. May I have your business card?

Steve: Sure. Here you are. [Hands Darren a card] Do you have a card?

Darren: No, sorry. I haven't been given any yet.

Amanda: You'll receive your cards later this week, Darren. Let me introduce you to some other staff members. Brenda is our foreign <u>consultant</u>. Brenda, this is Darren Jiang. Darren, this is Brenda Hillsbury.

Brenda: Hello, Darren. Which department are you in?

Darren: I'm in engineering. So, as a foreign consultant, what do you do at WHT?

Brenda: Well, my duties include giving advice when dealing with <u>overseas</u> clients, doing research, and meeting clients when they come to Taiwan.

今天是達倫‧江到王氏、蕭氏暨童氏事務所（簡稱 WHT）這家台灣工程公司任職的第一天。WHT 的人事經理艾曼達‧夏普正在將達倫介紹給 WHT 其他的職員認識。

艾曼達：史提夫‧馮，我介紹達倫‧江給你認識。今天是達倫到職的第一天。

史提夫：嗨，達倫，很高興認識你。我負責 WHT 歐洲的專案。很高興你能加入公司。

達倫：　謝謝，史提夫，非常高興認識你。可以跟你要一張名片嗎？

史提夫：當然，喏。（遞一張名片給達倫）你有名片嗎？

達倫：　沒有，抱歉，他們還沒給我。

艾曼達：本週稍後你就會拿到你的名片，達倫。讓我幫你介紹其他幾個同事。布蘭達是我們的外籍顧問。布蘭達，這位是達倫‧江。達倫，這位是布蘭達‧希斯貝里。

布蘭達：你好，達倫。你在哪個部門？

達倫：　我在工程部。那，身為外籍顧問，妳在 WHT 都做些什麼？

布蘭達：呃，我的職責包括與海外客戶打交道時提供意見、做研究，並在客戶來台時與他們會面。

Ⓦord List

personnel [ˌpɝsŋˋɛl] *adj.* 人事的；負責人事的
consultant [kənˋsʌltŋt] *n.* （提供意見的）專家；顧問
overseas [ˋovɚˋsiz] *adj.* 海外的；外國的

2.1 繼續介紹 More Introductions

Amanda takes Darren to the sales department and continues to introduce him to the staff.

Amanda: Everyone, I'd like you to welcome Darren to the company.

Paul: Hi Darren. <u>Welcome aboard</u>. I've worked for WHT for eight years. What will you be doing for WHT?

Darren: I work in the engineering department.

Paul: Where did you work before?

Darren: I was with MegaProjects Ltd. for three years.

Paul: Wow, that's a great company. Hey, Sarah, come over here and say hello to Darren. It's his first day on the job.

Sarah: Nice to meet you.

Paul: Darren used to be with MegaProjects Ltd.

Sarah: I've heard MegaProjects is a good company to work for.

Darren: Yes, it is. However, I think WHT offers me more opportunity. What do you do for WHT, Sarah?

Sarah: I'm in sales, just like Paul. May I give you my card?

Darren: Please — that would be great. I look forward to working with you.

Sarah: Me, too.

艾曼達帶達倫到業務部門，繼續把他介紹給員工們認識。

艾曼達：各位，我想請人家歡迎達倫加入公司。

保羅：　嗨，達倫，歡迎加入。我已經在 WHT 工作八年了。你在 WHT 會做哪方面的事務？

達倫：　我在工程部工作。

保羅：　你以前在哪裡做事？

達倫：　我之前在鴻大專案有限公司做了三年。

保羅：　哇！那家公司很不錯呢。嘿，莎拉，過來跟達倫打聲招呼，今天是他到職的第一天。

莎拉：　很高興認識你。

保羅：　達倫以前在鴻大專案有限公司。

莎拉：　我聽說在鴻大專案公司工作很不錯。

達倫：　是的，的確是，不過我覺得 WHT 提供我更多的機會。妳在 WHT 做些什麼，莎拉？

莎拉：　我在業務部，跟保羅一樣。我給你我的名片好嗎？

達倫：　那再好不過了，麻煩妳。我很期待能夠與妳共事。

莎拉：　我也是。

ord List
....
welcome aboard 歡迎加入；歡迎搭乘

3 Biz 加分句型 Nice-to-Know Phrases

3.1 交換名片 Exchanging Business Cards

 track 04

❶ May I have your business card?
我可以跟你要張名片嗎？

> 例 May I have your business card, David?
>
> 我可以跟你要張名片嗎，大衛？

❷ Sorry, I'm out (of cards).
抱歉，我（名片）用完了。

> 例 Sorry, I'm out. Let me write my number down for you.
>
> 抱歉，我用完了。讓我把我的號碼寫下來給你。

❸ Here's my (business) card.
這是我的名片。

> 例 Hi, I'm Andy. Here's my business card.
>
> 嗨，我是安迪，這是我的名片。

❹ Let me give you one of my new cards.
讓我給你一張我的新名片。

> 例 Fred, let me give you one of my new cards. My number has changed.
>
> 佛萊德，讓我給你一張我的新名片。我的號碼換了。

 ord List

business cards [ˋbɪznɪsˏkɑrd] *n.* 名片

3.2 歡迎新員工 Welcoming New Employees

❶ Welcome aboard.
歡迎加入。
例 Welcome aboard, Jim!
歡迎加入，吉姆。

❷ It's good to have you in/with the company.
很高興你能加入公司。
例 It's nice to meet you, Betty. It's good to have you in the company.
很榮幸認識妳，貝蒂。很高興妳能加入公司。

❸ Good to have you with us.
很高興你能加入我們。
例 Good to have you with us, Bob.
很高興你能加入我們，鮑伯。

❹ I look forward to working with you.
我很期待能夠與你共事。
例 I look forward to working with you, Sarah.
我很期待能夠與妳共事，莎拉。

ord List
....
look forward to + Ving 期待……

:::::::::: 小心陷阱 ::::::::::

☹ 錯誤用法：

I **work** for this company for 10 years.

我已經在這家公司工作十年了。

☺ 正確用法：

I **have worked** for this company for 10 years.

我已經在這家公司工作十年了。

:::::::::: Biz 一點通 ::::::::::

There are some questions you should <u>avoid</u> asking when meeting people, even if you are <u>curious</u> about the answer. One question you should never ask, especially if you don't know the person quite well, is "How much money do you make?" Other questions that may seem too personal, especially on your first day at work are "Do you like your job?" and "Are you married?"

與人初次見面時，就算你很好奇想知道某些問題的答案，也應該避免問這些問題。一個絕對不應該問的問題（特別是如果你跟這個人並不熟的話），就是「你的薪水多少？」，其他有可能顯得太私人的問題（特別是如果你是第一天到職的話），則是「你喜歡你的工作嗎？」和「你結婚了嗎？」。

Ⓦord List

avoid [əˋvɔɪd] *v.* 避免（做……）

curious [ˋkjurɪəs] *adj.* 好奇心強的；愛打聽的

4　實戰演練 Practice Exercises

I　請為下列詞語選出最適合本章的中文譯義。

❶ I'm in sales.

(A) 我在業務部。　(B) 我在打折。　(C) 我待價而沽。

❷ Welcome aboard.

(A) 歡迎加入。　(B) 請登船。　(C) 歡迎歸國。

❸ day shift

(A) 日間班車　(B) 早班　(C) 更改日期

II　你會如何回應下面這兩句話？

❶ Good to have you with the company.

(A) Yes, it is a good company.

(B) Thank you.

(C) It's nice to meet you, too.

❷ May I give you my business card?

(A) Sure, thanks.

(B) Here you are.

(C) I'm sorry, I don't have a business card.

III　請用下列詞語寫出一篇簡短的對話。

I'd like you to meet	I'm in
I'm responsible for	is new to the company
Do you have a card?	It's good to have you in the company.

＊解答請見 226 頁

第 2 章

規劃安排
Making Arrangements

Setting times for meetings and other employee get-togethers is a frequent and fundamental aspect of the workplace. Coordinating dates and times can be difficult, especially if both parties are busy. Being flexible and willing to compromise can be very useful in deciding on a time that is mutually agreeable. Of course, there are times when you can't compromise on a certain date, and other times when you must change plans you previously made.

安排會議和其他員工聚會的時間在工作場所中是一個頻繁而重要的面向。協調日期和時間並不容易，尤其是如果雙方都很忙的話。能保有彈性且願意作出讓步，對訂出一個雙方都認可的時間十分有幫助。當然，會有些時候你無法在某一個日期上讓步，還有些時候你必須變更之前已訂好的計畫。

Biz 必通句型 Need-to-Know Phrases

 track 05

1.1 安排時間和日期 Arranging Times and Dates

❶ **Can you tell me when you are <u>available</u>?**
可不可以告訴我你何時有空？
例 Hi Bob, can you tell me when you are available this week?
嗨，鮑伯，可不可以告訴我你這星期何時有空？

❷ **When is convenient for you?**
你什麼時候方便？
例 I'd like to talk to you about the project. When is convenient for you?
我想跟你談談這個專案。你什麼時候方便？

❸ **Do you have any free time on (day)?**
你（日期）有空嗎？
例 Do you have any free time on Tuesday or Wednesday?
你星期二或星期三有空嗎？

❹ **What is your schedule like (time)?**
你（時間）的行程是如何安排的？
例 Cindy, what is your schedule like next week?
辛蒂，妳下星期的行程是如何安排的？

 ord List

available [əˋveləbl] *adj.* 有空的

❺Are you free (on a day/at a time)?

你（日期／時間）有空嗎？

例 Are you free on Friday afternoon?

你星期五下午有空嗎？

❻Why don't we <u>make</u> it (day/time)?

我們何不約在（日期／時間）？

例 About the meeting, why don't we make it Thursday?

我們何不把開會時間約在星期四？

❼Is (day/time) OK with you?

你（日期／時間）可以嗎？

例 Is next Wednesday morning OK with you, Shelly?

妳下星期三早上可以嗎，榭莉？

❽What about (day/time)?

（日期／時間）如何？

例 What about tomorrow or the day after?

明天或後天如何？

 ord List

....

make [mek] *v.* 安排見面；赴約

1.2 同意與拒絕時間 Agreeing to and Rejecting Times

❶ That's a good time for me.（無條件同意）
我那個時間可以。
> 例 Yes, no problem. That's a good time for me.
> 好，沒問題，我那個時間可以。

❷ That sounds fine.（無條件同意）
應該沒問題。
> 例 Tuesday at 3 p.m. That sounds fine.
> 星期二下午三點應該沒問題。

❸ Let me check my schedule first.（稍後再作出決定）
讓我先看一下我的時間表。
> 例 Let me check my schedule first and then call you back.
> 讓我先看一下我的時間表再回你電話。

❹ Can I get back to you on that?（稍後再作出決定）
我可以再告訴你嗎？
> 例 I'm not sure right now. Can I get back to you on that later today?
> 我現在還不確定。我可以今天稍後再告訴你嗎？

Word List
reject [rɪ`dʒɛkt] *v.* 拒絕；否決

❺ I'm sorry. I'm busy at that time.（有禮貌地拒絕）
很抱歉，我那個時間有事。

例 I'm sorry. I'm busy at that time, Doris.
很抱歉，我那個時間有事，桃樂絲。

❻ I'm afraid that won't work for me.（有禮貌地拒絕）
那個時間我恐怕不行。

例 I'm very busy on Wednesday, so I'm afraid that won't work for me.
我星期三非常忙，所以那個時間我恐怕不行。

❼ Can we make it another time?（建議改約其他時間）
我們可不可以改約另一個時間？

例 Can we make it another time? Monday at 1:30 perhaps?
我們可不可以改約另一個時間？比方說星期一的一點半？

❽ That time's impossible for me.（斷然拒絕）
那個時間我完全沒辦法。

例 Monday morning at 9 o'clock? That time's impossible for me.
星期一早上九點？那個時間我完全沒辦法。

 Word **L**ist
I'm afraid + (that) 子句　我恐怕……

2 實戰會話 Show Time

2.1 安排重要會議
Scheduling an Important Meeting

 track 06

WHT's head of engineering, Simon Liu, is <u>holding an important meeting</u> to talk about a huge engineering project to be <u>constructed</u> in Europe. He has asked his personal secretary, Penny Kuo, to call the engineers and other people <u>involved</u> in the project to find out when they are available for the meeting.

Penny: Good afternoon, Steve. The reason I'm calling is that Mr. Liu would like to hold a meeting to discuss the big European project this week. Can you tell me when you are available this week?

Steve: I think Tuesday or Wednesday would be best for me.

Penny: When is convenient for you on Tuesday?

Steve: In the afternoon is most convenient, between 2 and 4 o'clock.

Penny: Thank you, Steve. I'll get back to you after I contact the others.

Penny contacts Darren.

Darren: Hello, this is Darren speaking.

Penny: Hi Darren, this is Penny, Mr. Liu's secretary. I'm calling about a meeting Mr. Liu wants to have about the European project. What is your schedule like on Tuesday afternoon?

Darren: That's a good time for me.

Penny: Great — I'll call you later to <u>confirm</u> the time.

Penny contacts Brenda Hillsbury.

Penny: Hello Brenda, this is Penny. Mr. Liu has called an important meeting to discuss the European construction project. Are you free on Tuesday afternoon?

Brenda: Let me check my schedule first. Let's see... hmm... I'm sorry, I'm busy at that time. Wednesday would be much better for me.

Penny: OK, I will let Mr. Liu know that. I'll talk to you later about this, Brenda. Bye for now.

譯 文

WHT 的工程部主管賽門‧劉要召開一場重要的會議，討論一項將在歐洲進行的重大工程專案。他已經請他的私人秘書潘妮‧郭打電話給工程師和其他與專案有關的人員，看他們何時有空開會。

潘妮： 午安，史提夫。我打電話過來因為劉先生想要在這星期開會討論那個歐洲的大專案。能不能告訴我你這週何時有空？

史提夫：我想星期二或星期三對我會最方便。

潘妮： 你星期二何時方便呢？

史提夫：下午兩點到四點之間最方便。

潘妮： 謝謝你，史提夫。我先去聯絡其他人，回頭再通知你。

潘妮和達倫聯絡。

達倫： 喂，我是達倫。

潘妮： 嗨，達倫，我是劉先生的秘書潘妮。我打電話過來想和你討論一下劉先生要召開的一個有關歐洲專案的會議。你星期二下午的時間是如何安排的？

達倫： 我那時間可以。

潘妮： 好極了，那我等會兒再打給你確認一下時間。

潘妮跟布蘭達‧希斯貝里聯絡。

潘妮： 喂，布蘭達，我是潘妮。劉先生決定召開一個重要會議，討論那個歐洲建築工程的專案。妳星期二下午有空嗎？

布蘭達：讓我先看一下我的時間表。我看看……嗯……抱歉，我那時間有事。星期三對我會方便得多。

潘妮： 好，我會讓劉先生知道這狀況。我之後再跟妳討論這件事，布蘭達，就先這樣了。

Word List

hold/call a meeting 召開會議

construct [kən`strʌkt] *v.* 建設；建造

involved [ɪn`vɑlvd] *adj.* 有關係的

confirm [kən`fɝm] *v.* 確認

2.2 安排時間上的難題 Scheduling Problems

Steve and Darren realize they have another <u>commitment</u> on Tuesday afternoon. Penny is forced to try to <u>reschedule</u> the meeting.

Steve: Penny, I have to apologize to you. I forgot that I have another big meeting <u>concerning</u> another project on Tuesday afternoon.

Penny: That's alright, Steve. Brenda also has problems with that time as well. I will check with Mr. Liu about rescheduling a new time for the meeting. I'll call you back on that later today.

Darren calls Penny.

Darren: Penny, I'm really sorry, but I need to change the time. I didn't realize that I had another meeting with Steve about another project on Tuesday.

Penny: That's OK, Darren. Steve just told me about that. We will reschedule the time of the new meeting.

Penny talks with Mr. Liu about a new meeting time and comes up with Wednesday at 1:30 p.m.

Penny: Hi again, Steve. Mr. Liu has <u>proposed</u> a new time for the meeting. Is Wednesday at 1:30 p.m. OK with you?

Steve: That sounds fine. So, that's Wednesday afternoon at 1:30, right?

Penny: That's right, Steve. Thanks. I'll let the others know. Goodbye.

譯文

史提夫和達倫想到他們在星期二下午另外有事，潘妮被迫要試著重新安排開會時間。

史提夫：潘妮，我得跟妳道歉。我忘了我星期二下午要開另一個關於另一項專案的重要會議。

潘妮：　沒關係，史提夫，布蘭達那個時間也不行。我會再跟劉先生確認是否要另訂一個開會時間。我今天稍後會再打給你討論這件事情。

達倫打電話給潘妮。

達倫：　潘妮，真對不起，我需要改時間。我之前沒想到我星期二和史提夫要開另一個專案的會議。

潘妮：　沒關係，達倫，史提夫剛才打過電話告訴我這件事。我們會重訂會議時間。

潘妮和劉先生討論新的開會時間，並將時間訂在星期三下午一點半。

潘妮：　嗨，又是我，史提夫。劉先生提了一個新的開會時間。你星期三下午一點半可以嗎？

史提夫：應該沒問題。所以是星期三下午一點半，對吧？

潘妮：　沒錯，史提夫。謝謝。我會通知其他人，再見。

ord List

commitment [kə`mɪtmənt] *n.* 約定

reschedule [ri`skɛdʒʊl] *v.* 重新排定……的時間

concerning [kə`sɜnɪŋ] *prep.* 關於（＝about）

propose [prə`poz] *v.* 提出；提議

3 Biz 加分句型 Nice-to-Know Phrases

 track 07

3.1 確認與查驗計畫
Confirming and Checking Plans

❶ Great, see you (day and time), then.（當你知道日期和時間時）
好極了，那我們（日期和時間）見。
例 Great, see you on Thursday at 10 a.m., then.
好極了，那我們星期四早上十點見。

❷ So, that's (date and time), right?（確認）
所以是（日期和時間），對吧？
例 So, that's Friday afternoon at 2:30, right?
所以是星期五下午兩點半，對吧？

❸ You said (date and time), but did you mean (date and time)?（懷疑有錯時）
你說（日期和時間），但是你是不是指（日期和時間）？
例 You said Wednesday, July 10th at 1 p.m., but did you mean Wednesday, July 12th?
你說七月十日星期三下午一點，但是你是不是指七月十二日星期三？

❹ Can you say the date again for me?（當你不確定時間時）
可不可以請你再說一次日期？
例 Excuse me. Can you say the date again for me?
對不起，可不可以請你再說一次日期？

3.2 變更時間 Making Changes

❶ I forgot that (sth. to do).
我忘了（有某件事要做）。
例 Oops, I forgot that I have another appointment at that time.
糟糕，我忘了我那時間另外有約。

❷ I didn't realize that (sth. to do).
我之前沒想到（有某件事要做）。
例 I'm sorry, I didn't realize that I have a meeting on that day.
對不起，我之前沒想到我那天要開會。

❸ Something has come up.（用於稍後出現了更重要的事情時）
我臨時有事。
例 Pete, <u>forgive</u> me, something has come up and I can't make that date anymore.
彼特，對不起，我臨時有事，那天我沒辦法。

❹ Sorry, I need to change the time.
抱歉，我需要改時間。
例 Sorry, Sue, I need to change the time of our meeting.
抱歉，蘇，我需要更改我們開會的時間。

 ord List
....
forgive [fɚ`gɪv] v. 原諒

::::::::: 小心陷阱 :::::::::

☹ 錯誤用法：

That's **good time** for me.

我那個時間可以。

☺ 正確用法：

That's **a good time** for me.

我那個時間可以。

::::::::: **Biz 一點通** :::::::::

Remember that politeness is always an important factor in making arrangements, especially when you can't make a time that was suggested by another person, or when you have to call back and change plans. Phrases such as "I'm really sorry," and "Please forgive me," can be quite helpful in <u>maintaining</u> a good relationship with your colleagues. A willingness to be <u>flexible</u> and possibly make changes in your schedule is also useful in reaching an agreement on dates and times.

記住，規劃安排時保持禮貌永遠都是很重要的，尤其是當其他人提出的時間你不方便，或是你必須回電更改計畫時。「真的很抱歉」和「請原諒」這類用語十分有助於和同事維繫良好的關係。如果你樂意配合，還能進而調整自己的時間，也同樣有助於雙方在訂出日期和時間上達成共識。

 Word **L**ist

maintain [men`ten] *v.* 維持；養護

flexible [`flɛksəbl] *adj.* 有彈性的

4 實戰演練 Practice Exercises

I 請為下列詞語選出最適合本章的中文譯義。

❶ make arrangements

(A) 裝飾布置 (B) 協商解決 (C) 規劃安排

❷ Something has come up.

(A) 有東西跑出來。 (B) 臨時有事。 (C) 有東西困擾我。

❸ call a meeting

(A) 開始一場會議 (B) 命名一場會議 (C) 召開一場會議

II 你會如何回應下面這兩句話？

❶ When is convenient for you?

(A) I'm busy.

(B) Wednesday morning is good for me.

(C) That sounds fine.

❷ Can we make it another time?

(A) Sure, no problem.

(B) It's 11 o'clock in the morning.

(C) Great, see you then.

III 請用下列詞語寫出一篇簡短的對話。

What is your schedule like (time)?   free time

That sounds fine.   I didn't realize

Why don't we make it (time)?   So, that's (date and time), right?

＊解答請見 227 頁

談論專案與任務
Talking About Projects
And Assignments

Discussions about projects and timelines are a common feature in almost every kind of business. It's essential to properly convey requirements in a clear, concise manner. The consequences of misunderstanding and miscommunication in this area can be severe. Clearly stating objectives and deadlines, making suggestions, giving opinions, and making sure everyone knows their duties are the foundations of success for any project.

幾乎每一種行業都有一個共通點，那就是討論專案和最後期限。用清楚、扼要的方式貼切地傳達各項要求十分重要。在這方面若發生誤解和辭不達意的狀況，後果可能會非常嚴重。清楚地陳述目標與期限、提出建議、提供意見，並確保每個人明瞭自己的職責為何，是任何專案成功的基石。

1 Biz 必通句型 Need-to-Know Phrases

 track 08

1.1 討論職責和期限
Discussing Responsibilities and Deadlines

❶ **(Name) take care of....**
（姓名）負責……。
例 Jim will take care of <u>updating</u> the sales reports.
吉姆會負責更新業務報告。

❷ **(Name) deal with....**
（姓名）處理……。
例 Simone deals with clients from all over the world.
席夢處理世界各地的客戶。

❸ **(Name) <u>is responsible to</u>....**
（姓名）向……負責。
例 Laura is responsible to the marketing manager.
蘿拉向行銷經理負責。

❹ **The deadline for... is....**
……的最後期限是……。
例 The deadline for this report is October 20th.
這份報告的最後期限是十月二十日。

 Word **List**

update [ʌpˋdet] v. 更新

be responsible to + sb. 向……負責

❺ ...must be done by (time).

……必須在（時間）前完成。

例 This assignment must be done by 5 o'clock tomorrow.

這項任務必須在明天五點前完成。

❻ The <u>cutoff</u> date for... is....

……的截止日期是……。

例 The cutoff date for this project is the end of August.

這項專案的截止日期是八月底。

❼ ...is ahead of schedule.

……的進度超前。

例 Good news! We're two weeks ahead of schedule.

好消息！我們的進度超前了兩個禮拜。

❽ ...is behind schedule.

……的進度落後。

例 Because we're behind schedule so much, we have to work overtime.

因為我們的進度嚴重落後，所以我們必須加班。

ord List

cutoff [ˋkʌtˏɔf] n. 【會計】結算日；切斷

1.2 提出意見與建議 Offering Opinions and Suggestions

❶ In my opinion,....
依我看，……。

例 In my opinion, we should delay this project by one month.

依我看，我們應該把這個專案延後一個月。

❷ In my view,....
依我看，……。

例 In my view, this is not a good idea.

依我看，這不是個好主意。

❸ I strongly think....（強烈表達意見）
我深切認為……。

例 I strongly think this is the product we should <u>promote</u>.

我深切認為這是我們應該促銷的產品。

❹ It might be a good idea to....（溫和表達意見）
……也許是個好主意。

例 It might be a good idea to <u>lower</u> the price.

降價也許是個好主意。

Ｗord List

promote [prə`mot] *v.* 促銷（商品）

lower [`loɚ] *v.* 降低（價格、程度等）

❺ I suggest....

我建議……。

例 I suggest we hire another person.

我建議我們再雇一個人。

❻ Why don't you...?

你何不……？

例 Why don't you make a list of things that need to be done?

你何不把該做的事項列一張清單？

❼ You should....

你應該……。

例 You should get to the office earlier.

你應該早點到辦公室。

❽ We/You need to....

我們／你需要……。

例 We need to finish this assignment by tomorrow.

我們需要在明天之前完成這項任務。

ord List
....

make a list of sth. 為……列張清單

2 實戰會話 Show Time

2.1 專案會議（1）The Project Meeting I

 track 09

In order to prepare for WHT's large construction project in Germany, head engineer Simon Liu is holding a meeting. Among those in <u>attendance</u> are Steve Fong, Darren Jiang, and Brenda Hillsbury.

Simon: I'd like to talk today about the responsibilities for the project and the deadlines. First, Steve will take care of <u>filing</u> all the necessary documents with the German government for <u>approval</u>. Brenda, you will deal with any <u>translations</u> from German to English and Chinese.

Brenda: I have a question. When is the deadline for <u>submitting applications</u> to the government for this project?

Simon: Let's see... we've set March 1st as our cutoff date.

Brenda: In that case, I suggest that Steve start giving me the documents that need to be translated as soon as he finishes them.

Steve: Thanks for your suggestion, Brenda. I'll certainly do that as soon as possible.

Simon: Darren, you will be responsible to Steve on this project. Steve, you should meet with Darren tomorrow morning to discuss his duties further.

Steve: That's a great idea. Darren, why don't you meet me in my office at 9:30 a.m.?

Darren: I've got a training <u>session</u> from 9 until 11 tomorrow morning. It might be a good idea to meet tomorrow afternoon instead.

Steve: Sure.

為了準備 WHT 在德國的大型建築工程專案，總工程師賽門‧劉正在舉行一場會議。與會者有史提夫‧馮、達倫‧江和布蘭達‧希斯貝里。

賽門： 我今天想要談一下這項專案的職責和最後期限。首先，史提夫會負責向德國政府提出申請批准的所有必要文件。布蘭達，妳將處理所有德翻英和德翻中的翻譯。

布蘭達：我有個疑問。向政府提交這項專案申請的最後期限是什麼時候？

賽門： 我看看……我們訂的截止日期是三月一號。

布蘭達：這樣的話，我建議史提夫一完成需要翻譯的文件，就開始把它們陸續交給我。

史提夫：謝謝妳提的建議，布蘭達，我一定會儘快給妳。

賽門： 達倫，這個專案你要向史提夫負責。史提夫，明天早上你應該和達倫開個會進一步討論他的職責。

史提夫：好主意。達倫，你何不明天早上九點半到我辦公室來找我？

達倫： 我明天早上九點到十一點有個訓練課程。改在明天下午碰面也許是個好主意。

史提夫：當然。

attendance [əˋtɛndəns] *n.* 出席（人數）
file [faɪl] *v.* 存檔；正式提出
approval [əˋpruvl] *n.* 批准；認可
translation [trænsˋleʃən] *n.* 翻譯

submit [səbˋmɪt] *v.*（向……）提出……；呈遞
application [ˌæpləˋkeʃən] *n.* 申請；申請書
session [ˋsɛʃən] *n.* 授課（時間）

2.2 專案會議 (2)：進度報告
The Project Meeting II — Status Report

Three months after the <u>initial</u> meeting, the engineering team holds another important meeting to <u>assess</u> how the project is <u>proceeding</u>. Also attending the meeting is Laura Deng, another senior engineer.

Simon: OK, let's take a good look at this project and see where we are doing well and where we need some improvement. In my opinion, we only have a few problems. Steve, why don't you begin?

Steve: Thanks, Simon. In my view, we are ahead of schedule on many things. But there are a couple of areas where we are experiencing some problems. We need to work harder to make sure that the designs are finished in two months.

Laura: I don't think that's enough time. There are a lot of designs that still have to be completed. Is it possible to have an <u>extension</u>?

Simon: I'm very sorry, Laura, but the designs must be done in two months. If they aren't, that will put much of the rest of the project behind schedule.

Steve: We need to really hurry up on the designs. I strongly think we need to assign more people to work on the designs. I suggest letting Darren help with the designs.

Laura: I'm not sure that's a good idea. Darren is new to the company and hasn't had a lot of experience with these kinds of jobs.

Simon: I'm sorry. I disagree with you, Laura. Darren is a smart guy and we need the help with the designs.

譯文

第一次會議的三個月後，工程團隊召開另一次重要的會議來評估專案的進展。另一位資深工程師蘿拉‧鄧也出席了這次會議。

賽門： 好，我們仔細瞧瞧這項專案，看看我們哪裡做得不錯、哪裡需要改進。依我看，我們只有幾個問題。史提夫，你何不起個頭？

史提夫：謝謝，賽門。我認為我們在許多事情上都超前進度，但是在幾個方面遭遇了一些問題。我們需要趕工才能確保設計圖能在兩個月內完成。

蘿拉： 我覺得時間不夠，我們還有許多設計圖得完成。有可能延長期限嗎？

賽門： 很遺憾，蘿拉，但是設計圖必須在兩個月內完成。如果無法完成，就會讓專案接下來的其他部分的進度大幅落後。

史提夫：我們真的需要快快趕工完成設計圖。我深切認為我們需要加派人手來作設計圖。我建議讓達倫幫忙作設計圖。

蘿拉： 那恐怕不是個好主意。達倫才剛進公司，對這類工作的經驗還不是很多。

賽門： 抱歉，我不同意妳的看法，蘿拉。達倫是個聰明人，而我們需要人手幫忙作設計圖。

ord List

initial [ɪ`nɪʃəl] *adj.* 開始的；最初的
assess [ə`sɛs] *v.* 評估；評價
proceed [prə`sid] *v.* 著手進行
extension [ɪk`stɛnʃən] *n.* 延長

3 Biz 加分句型 Nice-to-Know Phrases

 track 10

3.1 要求更多時間 Asking for More Time

❶ Do you think you could give me more time?
你覺得你可以給我更多時間嗎？

例 Do you think you could give me more time to complete the project?
你覺得你可以給我更多時間來完成這項專案嗎？

❷ Is it possible to have an extension?
有可能延長期限嗎？

例 Is it possible to have an extension? I'm quite busy right now.
有可能延長期限嗎？我現在還滿忙的。

❸ I don't think that's enough time.
我覺得時間不夠。

例 Only two weeks? I don't think that's enough time to do a good job.
只有兩個禮拜？我覺得這樣的時間不夠把事情做好。

❹ I'm sorry, I won't be able to finish it by then.
抱歉，我沒辦法在那之前做完。

例 I'm sorry, I won't be able to finish it by then — it's too soon.
抱歉，我沒辦法在那之前做完 — 時間太趕了。

3.2 接受和拒絕建議 Accepting and Rejecting Advice

接受建議

❶ That's a great idea!
好主意！
例 That's a great idea! Thanks, Jim.
好主意！謝了，吉姆。

❷ Thanks for your suggestion.
謝謝你的建議。
例 Thanks for your suggestion, Irene.
謝謝妳的建議，艾琳。

拒絕建議

❸ I'm not sure that's a good idea.
那恐怕不是個好主意。
例 I'm not sure that's a good idea at this point.
現階段那恐怕不是個好主意。

❹ I'm sorry. I disagree.
抱歉，我不同意。
例 I'm sorry. I disagree with your suggestion.
抱歉，我不同意你的建議。

░░░░░░░ 小心陷阱 ░░░░░░░

☹ 錯誤用法：

I suggest you **to study** harder.

我建議你更用功一些。

☺ 正確用法：

I suggest you **study** harder.

我建議你更用功一些。

░░░░░░░ Biz 一點通 ░░░░░░░

Most people take deadlines very seriously—and for good reason. If you fail to meet a deadline, you risk being thought of as <u>unreliable</u>. Therefore, if you have any doubts about meeting a deadline, it's best to <u>raise your concerns</u> at the beginning, rather than later as the deadline approaches. If a deadline is unreasonable or impossible, then state your reasons clearly and early in the process.

大多數人都非常重視最後期限，而且有其充分的理由必須如此。如果你無法趕上最後期限，就有可能被認為是不可靠的。因此，如果你對趕上期限有所懷疑，應該在一開始就提出疑慮，而不要等到之後期限快到時才說。如果期限不合理或不可行，那就在事情進行的一開始便清楚說出你的理由。

Word List

risk [rɪsk] *v.* 冒⋯⋯的風險

unreliable [͵ʌnrɪˋlaɪəbl] *adj.* 不可靠的；不可信賴的

raise one's concerns 提出疑慮

4 　實戰演練 Practice Exercises

I 請為下列詞語選出最適合本章的中文譯義。

1 responsible to

(A) 負責……　(B) 向……負責　(C) 有擔當的

2 raise one's concerns

(A) 提高需求　(B) 增加……的利害關係　(C) 提出疑慮

3 cutoff date

(A) 停工日期　(B) 斷交日期　(C) 截止日期

II 你會如何回應下面這兩句話？

1 We are behind schedule on this project.

(A) That's great.

(B) No, it's in front of the project.

(C) Let's find a way to speed up.

2 It might be a good idea to get to work earlier.

(A) At 8 a.m.

(B) Thanks for the suggestion.

(C) I don't have any idea.

III 請用下列詞語寫出一篇簡短的對話。

deadline	I suggest
In my opinion	That's a great idea
must be done by	take care of

＊解答請見 228 頁

第 **4** 章

與人閒聊
Engaging in Small Talk

Of course, not every conversation at work is about schedules, dead-lines and important decisions. Social interactions with coworkers are an integral part of office life. The ability to make small talk can make your work-life more enjoyable and make others feel more comfortable when they are around you. Such social skills are also valued and often taken into consideration when promotions are handed out as well.

當然，不是所有工作時的對話都是在談論時間表、最後期限和重要決策。與同事社交互動是辦公室生活不可分割的一部分，能夠與同事閒聊可以讓你的職場生活更愉快，也可以讓別人與你相處時更自在。這種社交技巧相當重要，在拔擢升等時也經常會被列入考量。

1 Biz 必通句型 Need-to-Know Phrases

1.1 告知資訊與談論例行公事
Introducing Information and Talking About Routines

track 11

❶ Did you hear (information)?
你有沒有聽說（資訊）？
例 Did you hear that Stacey got a promotion?
你有沒有聽說史黛西升官了？

❷ Do you know (sth.)?
你知不知道（某事）？
例 Do you know if we will be getting any bonus this year?
你知不知道我們今年會不會拿到分紅？

❸ Someone told me (sth.).
有人告訴我（某事）。
例 Someone told me that we are getting new computers for the office. Is that true?
有人告訴我我們辦公室將會有新的電腦，是真的嗎？

❹ What do you do on your days off?
你休假的時候都做什麼？
例 Tell me Doris, what do you do on your days off?
告訴我，桃樂絲，妳休假的時候都做什麼？

 ord List

routine [ru`tɪn] *n.* 例行公事；日常工作　　　day off [`de ˌɔf] *n.* 休假日
bonus [`bonəs] *n.* 獎金；額外津貼

❺When are you taking a vacation?

你何時要休假？

例 When are you taking a vacation this year?

你今年何時要休假？

❻What are you doing this weekend?（星期五問）

你這個週末要做什麼？

例 I'm <u>curious</u> — what are you doing this weekend?

我很好奇，你這個週末要做什麼？

❼How was your weekend?（星期一或星期二問）

你的週末過得如何？

例 Hi Charlie. How was your weekend?

嗨，查理，你的週末過得如何？

❽How's work going these days?

最近工作如何？

例 How's work going these days, Wendy? Are you very busy?

最近工作如何，溫蒂？很忙嗎？

ord List

....

curious [ˋkjʊrɪəs] *adj.* 好奇的；渴望知道的

1.2 談論工作、個人經歷和提出邀請
Talking About Work, Personal History, and Making <u>Invitations</u>

❶ How long have you worked here?
你在這裡工作多久了？
例 How long have you worked here, Jasmine?
妳在這裡工作多久了，潔絲敏？

❷ What department are you in?
你在哪個部門？
例 Nice to meet you. What department are you in?
很高興認識你。你在哪個部門？

❸ Where did you work before?
你之前在哪裡工作？
例 So, where did you work before coming to this company?
那，你在來這家公司之前在哪裡工作？

❹ Where did you go to university?
你上的是哪一所大學？
例 I was wondering — where did you go to university?
我很好奇，你上的是哪一所大學？

 ord List

invitation [ɪnvəˋteʃən] *n.* 邀請

❺ What time do you (do sth.)?

你何時（做某事）？

例 What time do you usually get to work?

你通常何時來上班？

❻ Where's a good place (to do sth.)?（尋求建議）

有什麼好地方（做某事）？

例 Excuse me, where's a good place to have lunch around here?

對不起，請問附近有什麼好地方可以吃午餐？

❼ Would you like (to do sth.)?（提出邀請）

你要不要（做某事）？

例 Would you like to go for coffee sometime?

你要不要哪天去喝杯咖啡？

❽ How about (doing sth.)?（提出邀請）

（做某事）如何？

例 How about having lunch with me tomorrow?

明天和我一起吃午飯如何？

2 實戰會話 Show Time

2.1 茶水間閒聊 Chatting at the Water Cooler

 track 12

During a Monday afternoon coffee break, Darren meets Brenda and Paul at the water cooler.

Paul: Hey, you're the new guy, Darren, right? How's work going these days?

Darren: Pretty good, thanks. What department are you in?

Paul: I'm in sales. You've met Brenda before, haven't you?

Brenda: Oh yes, we've met. Hi, Darren. How was your weekend?

Darren: Not bad. I saw a movie and had some drinks with friends on Saturday night.

Brenda: Sounds fun. Someone told me you are originally from Boston. Did you grow up there?

Darren: Yes, I did.

Brenda: Where did you go to university?

Darren: M.I.T.

Brenda: You're kidding! That's a really great school.

Paul: Say, Brenda, did you hear the European project is behind schedule?

Brenda: Yes, I knew that. The designs are taking longer than expected.

Darren: Do you know if the delay will cause a lot of problems?

Brenda: I don't think so, as long as the designs are finished soon.

Paul: Well, you'd better be sure about that.

Darren: Hey, where's a good place to have lunch around here?

Brenda: There's a really good Italian restaurant about five minutes from here. There's also a pizza place around the corner.

Darren: Would you like to have lunch together later this week?

Brenda: Yes, thanks very much.

Paul: I'm sorry, I can't this week. I'm going out of town tomorrow. Maybe some other time.

 譯 文

在一個星期一下午的休息時間，達倫在飲水機旁碰到布蘭達和保羅。

保羅：　嘿，你是那個新來的，叫達倫，對不對？最近工作如何？

達倫：　還不錯，謝謝。你是哪個部門的？

保羅：　我在業務部。你見過布蘭達，對吧？

布蘭達：喔，是的，我們已經見過面了。嗨，達倫，你的週末過得如何？

達倫：　還不賴。我星期六晚上去看了場電影，還和朋友喝了幾杯。

布蘭達：聽起來滿好玩的。有人告訴我你是波士頓人。你是在那裡長大的嗎？

達倫：　是的，我在那兒長大。

布蘭達：你上的是哪一所大學？

達倫：　麻省理工學院。

布蘭達：真的假的！那所學校很棒耶。

保羅：　對了，布蘭達，妳有沒有聽說那個歐洲專案進度落後了？

布蘭達：有，我知道。設計圖花的時間比預期的要長。

達倫：　妳知不知道這樣延遲會不會造成很多問題？

布蘭達：只要設計圖快快完成，我想是不會的。

保羅：　嗯，你最好確定是那樣。

達倫：　嘿，附近有什麼好地方可以吃午餐？

布蘭達：有一家離這裡大約五分鐘路程的義大利餐廳很不錯。轉角那裡還有一家披薩店。

達倫：　二位這週稍後哪天要不要一起吃個午飯？

布蘭達：好，多謝。

保羅：　抱歉，我這週不行，我明天我有事要出城去。也許下一次吧。

2.2 午餐閒聊 Small Talk over Lunch

It's Friday, and Darren is having lunch with Brenda at the nice Italian restaurant near their office.

Darren: When are you taking a vacation this year, Brenda?

Brenda: In two months. I'm going to Greece and Italy.

Darren: Wow! I'm sure you'll have a wonderful time. How long have you worked at WHT? Where did you work before?

Brenda: For two years. Before working here, I was with an engineering consulting company in Toronto.

Darren: So, what do you do on your days off?

Brenda: I like to go hiking a lot. Also, I enjoy <u>cycling</u> and tennis. Of course, I sometimes go to the movies.

Darren: Where's a good place to go hiking? I like the <u>outdoors</u> as well. How about going hiking together sometime?

Brenda: I'd love to. What are you doing this weekend? Would you like to go then?

Darren: Yes, thanks very much.

Brenda: What time do you get up on the weekends?

Darren: Usually around 9 o'clock. How about meeting at 10:30?

Brenda: Sounds good.

今天是星期五，達倫和布蘭達在他們辦公室附近那家不錯的義大利餐廳共進午餐。

達倫： 妳今年何時要休假，布蘭達？

布蘭達：再兩個月。我要去希臘和義大利。

達倫： 哇！我想妳一定會玩得很開心。妳在 WHT 工作多久了？妳之前在哪裡工作？

布蘭達：兩年了。到這裡工作之前，我在多倫多的一家工程顧問公司。

達倫： 那，妳休假的時候都做什麼？

布蘭達：我很喜歡健行，也喜歡騎腳踏車和打網球。當然，有時候我會去看看電影。

達倫： 有什麼地方可以健行？我也喜歡到戶外。下次一起去健行如何？

布蘭達：我十分樂意。你這個週末要做什麼？要不要週末的時候去？

達倫： 好啊，多謝。

布蘭達：你週末都幾點起床？

達倫： 通常九點左右。十點半碰面如何？

布蘭達：好哇。

ord List

....

cycling [ˋsaɪk|ɪŋ] *n.* 騎腳踏車兜風

outdoors [ˋautˋdorz] *n.* 戶外；野外

3 Biz 加分句型 Nice-to-Know Phrases

3.1 回應新資訊 Responding to New Information track 13

❶ No, I hadn't heard that.
沒有，我沒聽說。
例 Bob got promoted? No, I hadn't heard that.
鮑伯升職了？沒有，我沒聽說。

❷ Yes, I knew that.
是的，我知道。
例 Yes, I knew that the boss is going to Egypt on holidays.
是的，我知道老闆要去埃及度假。

❸ That's interesting.
很有趣。
例 That's interesting — thanks for telling me.
很有趣，謝謝你告訴我。

❹ You're kidding! （聽到令人意外或驚奇的消息）
真的假的！
例 Jean got fired. You're kidding! Why?
珍被開除了。真的假的！為什麼？

3.2 回應邀請 Responding to Invitations

❶ I'd love to.（強力接受）
我十分樂意。
例 I'd love to go to lunch with you tomorrow.
我十分樂意明天和你共進午餐。

❷ Yes, thanks very much.
好，謝謝。
例 Yes, thanks very much for asking me.
好，多謝你邀請我。

❸ Maybe some other time.（有禮貌地拒絕）
也許下一次吧。
例 I'm pretty busy right now. Maybe some other time.
我現在挺忙的，也許下一次吧。

❹ I'm sorry, I can't.（有禮貌地拒絕）
對不起，我不行。
例 I'm sorry, I can't go for coffee until later.
對不起，我現在不能去喝咖啡，要等會兒。

::::::::: 小心陷阱 :::::::::

☹ 錯誤用法：

What do you do **on days off**?

你休假的時候都做什麼？

☺ 正確用法：

What do you do **on your days off**?

你休假的時候都做什麼？

::::::::: Biz 一點通 :::::::::

Need to <u>engage in</u> small talk? There are many suitable topics. Comments about the weather, as well as questions about a person's work background, hobbies and interests, family, and places he or she has traveled are all safe to chat about. Obviously, it's best to <u>steer clear of</u> <u>controversial</u> topics — especially with people you have just met — such as politics, race, religion, sex, and <u>sexuality</u>. As mentioned in Chapter 1, questions about salary should be avoided. Actually, avoiding money all together (e.g. "how much is your house worth?" or "how much did you pay for your car?") is probably a good idea.

需要和人閒聊嗎？有許多話題都十分合適。評論天氣、詢問一個人的工作背景、嗜好與興趣、家庭和他或她旅遊過的地方，都是安全的聊天話題。無庸贅言，最好不要碰觸爭議性的話題，例如政治、種族、宗教、性和性向，特別是不要跟才認識的人談這些。正如第一章提到的，應該避開有關薪水的問題。事實上，只要和錢有關的（例如「你的房子值多少錢？」或是「你的車子花了多少錢？」），最好都避開。

Word List

engage in sth...【消息】從事……；參與......

steer clear of【口語】避開……；與……不牽連

controversial [͵kɑntrəˋvɝʃəl] *adj.* 爭論的；引起爭論的

sexuality [͵sɛkʃʊˋælətɪ] *n.* 性向；性別

4　實戰演練 Practice Exercises

I　請為下列三題選出最適合本章的中文譯義。

❶ small talk

(A) 悄悄話　(B) 流言蜚語　(C) 閒聊

❷ How was your weekend?

(A) 你的週末過得如何？　(B)週末的時間你可以嗎？　(C)你在週末如何進行？

❸ steer clear of...

(A) 完全掌握……　(B) 避開……　(C) 和……劃清界限

II　你會如何回應下列這兩句話？

❶ How's work going these days?

(A) Pretty good, thanks.

(B) I take the bus.

(C) I'd love to.

❷ What time do you usually go for lunch?

(A) Yesterday I went for lunch at 12:30.

(B) At noon.

(C) No, I haven't had lunch yet.

III　請用下列詞語寫出一篇簡短的對話。

Did you hear?　　　　　　　　　　How about?

Where's a good place (to do sth.)?　Do you know?

How was your weekend?　　　　　Maybe some other time

＊解答請見 229 頁

第 **5** 章

保持談話熱度與結束談話
Maintaining and Ending Conversations

One common problem encountered in conversations — especially when it is with someone you don't know well — is not knowing how to keep the discussion flowing. Often after a few sentences, people go blank and don't know what to say. Such silences can be awkward and embarrassing. Another problem occurs when one of the participants has to or wants to quit the conversation, but isn't quite sure how to do it. Here are some phrases that will help you to overcome both difficulties.

談話時經常會碰到的一個問題就是不知如何讓討論持續進行,特別是當你和不熟的人聊天的時候。常常在聊了幾句後,大家就會無話可說,不知道接下來要談些什麼。這種沈默令人不自在又尷尬。另一個個問題則是,談話中的一方必須或想要退出談話時,不太確定該怎麼做。下面有一些詞語可幫助你克服這兩種困難。

1 Biz 必通句型 Need-to-Know Phrases

track 14

1.1 保持談話熱度
Keeping Conversations Going

❶ Tell me more (about sth.).（詢問更多資訊）
跟我多說一些（某事）。
例 Tell me more about your vacation.
跟我多說一些你度假的事。

❷ Then what happened?（追問更多資訊）
然後呢？
例 So, you ran out of gas this morning — then what happened?
那，你今天早上汽油用完了，然後呢？

❸ Really?（表達驚訝與興趣）
真的？
例 You got a promotion? Really? That's <u>fantastic</u>.
你升官了？真的？那太好了。

❹ You don't say?（表達驚訝與興趣）
是喔？
例 You're moving to the U.S. You don't say?
你要搬到美國去？是喔？

ord List

fantastic [fæn`tæstɪk] adj.【口語】極好的；很棒的

❺Are you sure?（質疑正確性）

你確定嗎？

例 Are you sure it's going to rain this afternoon?

你確定今天下午會下雨嗎？

❻Why is/was that?（詢問理由）

為什麼？

例 You're mad at your <u>supervisor</u>? Why is that?

你在生你主管的氣？為什麼？

❼What about you?（詢問意見或評論）

那你呢？

例 I think I'll take holidays in August. What about you?

我想我八月的時候要休假。你呢？

❽Oh yeah? / Uh-huh.（表達興趣）

是嗎？／嗯哼。

例 Oh yeah? You bought a computer yesterday? What kind?

是嗎？你昨天買了一個新電腦？哪一種？

ord List

supervisor [ˌsupɚˋvaɪzɚ] *n.* 主管；管理人

1.2 結束談話 Ending Conversations

❶ It was nice talking to you.
很高興和你聊天。
> 例 It was nice talking to you, Jim. See you later.
> 很高興和你聊天，吉姆。回頭見。

❷ Good to see you again
很高興又見到你。
> 例 Good to see you again, Amanda. Bye.
> 很高興又見到妳，艾曼達。拜拜。

❸ Well, I guess I should go.
嗯，我想我該走了。
> 例 Well, I guess I should go. Take care, Nancy.
> 嗯，我想我該走了。保重，南茜。

❹ Give me a call sometime. / I'll give you a call sometime.
改天打個電話給我。／我改天會打個電話給你。
> 例 Give me a call sometime, Steve. Have a nice day.
> 改天打個電話給我，史提夫。祝你今天過得愉快。

⑤ Sorry, I've got to go now. （表示緊急）
抱歉，我現在得走了。

例 Sorry, Tina, I've got to go now.
抱歉，提娜，我現在得走了。

⑥ I have another appointment to go to. （表示緊急）
我還有另一個約要赴。

例 Please excuse me. I have another appointment to go to.
真是不好意思，我還有另一個約要赴。

⑦ I really must be going. （表示更迫切的緊急）
我真的得走了。

例 I'm sorry. I really must be going right now.
對不起，我現在真的得走了。

⑧ I hate to <u>interrupt</u> you, but I have to leave now. （當某人還在講話時）
我很不願意打斷你，但是我現在得離開了。

例 David, I hate to interrupt you, but I have to leave now. See you later.
大衛，我很不願意打斷你，但是我現在得離開了。回頭見。

 ord List
....
interrupt [ˌɪntəˋrʌpt] v. 打斷（談話或講話者）

2 實戰會話 Show Time

2.1 在訓練研討會上 At the Training <u>Seminar</u>

 track 15

Darren is attending a training seminar along with a few other new employees at WHT. The seminar has just ended and Darren is speaking with fellow employee Sandra Chow.

Darren: Hi Sandra. Do you have time to talk right now?

Sandra: Sure.

Darren: What did you think of the seminar?

Sandra: It was OK, but not as good as the one I had for my previous job.

Darren: You don't say? Tell me more.

Sandra: Well, the speaker at that training seminar was fantastic — very <u>knowledgeable</u> and... he was a great speaker.

Darren: Uh-huh. When was that training?

Sandra: I'm sorry, I can't remember. But he took the time to make sure we understood everything very clearly. What about you? What did you think of the speaker?

Darren: I thought he was pretty good. I remember once I had a terrible training session. The speaker couldn't explain things clearly and he <u>spilled</u> coffee all over his notebook computer.

Sandra: Really? Then what happened?

Darren: Then the computer didn't work and he had to stop his presentation.

Sandra: That sounds pretty bad. Well, I guess I should go. It was nice talking to you.

Darren: I'll give you a call some time.

Sandra: OK, great.

達倫和其他幾個 WHT 的新員工一起參加訓練研討會。研討會剛剛結束，達倫正在和同事珊德拉‧周講話。

達倫：　嗨，珊德拉。妳現在有時間說話嗎？

珊德拉：有。

達倫：　妳覺得這場研討會怎樣？

珊德拉：還可以，但是沒有像我做前一份工作時參加的那一場那麼好。

達倫：　是喔？多告訴我一些。

珊德拉：嗯，那場訓練研討會的講者非常棒——很有學養……他是一個很不錯的講者。

達倫：　嗯哼。那場訓練是什麼時候的事？

珊德拉：對不起，我不記得了。他花了一些時間確定我們把所有的東西都弄得一清二楚。你呢？你覺得這個講者如何？

達倫：　我覺得他還不錯。我記得我曾經參加過一次很糟的訓練課程。那名講者東西解釋得不清不楚的，還把咖啡灑在他的筆記型電腦上。

珊德拉：真的啊？然後呢？

達倫：　然後電腦就壞了，他也不得不中止授課。

珊德拉：聽起來滿糟的。嗯，我想我該走了，很高興和你聊天。

達倫：　我改天再打個電話給妳。

珊德拉：好，好極了。

seminar [ˋsɛmə͵nɑr] *n.* 研討會；研討會課程

knowledgeable [ˋnɑlɪdʒəbl] *adj.* 有學問的；知識豐富的

spill [spɪl] *v.* 使溢出；灑

2.2 週一碰面閒聊 Monday Morning Chitchat

After a nice weekend, Darren and the other employees at WHT are back at work. Darren sees Paul in the hallway and is eager to chat with him and make a good impression.

Darren: Hi Paul. How was your weekend?

Paul: Oh, pretty good. What about you?

Darren: Fine, thanks. I did some hiking, saw a movie — it was great.

Paul: Oh yeah? Who did you go hiking with?

Darren: Brenda, the consultant from Canada.

Paul: Really? I didn't know you two were such good friends already. Be careful.

Darren: Why is that?

Paul: Many times office romances can be a problem. If you start dating and then break up, it will be emotionally difficult to see each other everyday at the office.

Darren: It's OK. We're just friends.

Paul: Are you sure? Did you say anything to make her think you wanted to be her boyfriend?

Darren: I'm not sure. I don't think so.

Paul: Anyway, like I said — be careful. Sorry, I've got to go right now. I've got another appointment.

Darren: OK, it was nice talking to you.

Just as Paul leaves, Brenda comes walking down the hallway and sees Darren.

Brenda: Hi Darren! Are you busy now?

Darren: Well, I should...

Brenda: Did you hear there's a new French restaurant that opened up near here? I was...

Darren: Brenda, I hate to interrupt you, but I have to leave now.

Brenda: Oh, OK. Good to see you again, anyway.

譯 文

在過了一個愉快的週末後，達倫和 WHT 的其他員工回到工作崗位上。達倫在走道上看到保羅，他迫不及待地想要和他聊聊，好給他留下好印象。

達倫：　嗨，保羅。你的週末過得如何？

保羅：　喔，還不錯。你呢？

達倫：　很好，謝謝。我去健了行，還看了場電影──還滿不錯的。

保羅：　喔，是嗎？你和誰去健行？

達倫：　布蘭達，加拿大來的顧問。

保羅：　真的啊？我不曉得你們兩個交情已經這麼好了。你要小心。

達倫：　為什麼？

保羅：　辦公室戀情常常都會很麻煩。如果你們開始交往又分手了，要每天在辦公室見到彼此，在情感上相當困難。

達倫：　沒事兒，我們只是朋友。

保羅：　你確定嗎？你有沒有說什麼讓她覺得你想當她男朋友的話？

達倫：　我不確定。我想沒有。

保羅：　不管怎樣，就像我說的，要小心。抱歉，我現在得走了，我還有另一個約。

達倫：　好，很高興和你聊天。

保羅才剛離開，布蘭達就朝走道這邊走來，她看到了達倫。

布蘭達：嗨，達倫！你現在在忙嗎？

達倫：　嗯，我應該……

布蘭達：你有沒有聽說這附近開了一家新的法國餐廳？我剛……

達倫：　布蘭達，我很不願意打斷妳，但是我現在得離開了。

布蘭達：喔，好，不過還是很高興又見到你。

chitchat [ˈtʃɪt.tʃæt] *n./v.* 聊天；閒談

consultant [kənˈsʌltn̩t] *n.* 提供意見的專家；顧問

office romance 辦公室戀情

break up (with sb.) （和某人）分手

3 Biz 加分句型 Nice-to-Know Phrases

3.1 確認某人是否有時間談話
Checking if the Person Has Time to Talk

❶ Do you have time to talk right now?
你現在有時間說話嗎？
> 例 Excuse me. Do you have time to talk right now?
> 對不起，你現在有時間說話嗎？

❷ Is now a good time to talk?
現在方便說話嗎？
> 例 Hi Betty. Is now a good time to talk?
> 嗨，貝蒂。現在方便說話嗎？

❸ Do you have a minute?
可以耽誤一點時間嗎？
> 例 Do you have a minute to discuss something, Bill?
> 可以耽誤你一點時間討論一下事情嗎，比爾？

❹ Are you busy?
你在忙嗎？
> 例 Are you busy, Laura? I'd like to talk to you.
> 妳在忙嗎，蘿拉？我想和妳說幾句話。

3.2 回答你不知道的事 Answering When You Don't Know

❶ I'm not sure (about sth.).
（某事）我不確定。
例 I'm not sure about that. Sorry.
那件事我不確定，抱歉。

❷ I really don't know (sth.).
我真的不知道（某事）。
例 I really don't know when Joe quit.
我真的不知道喬是什麼時候辭職的。

❸ I can't remember (sth.).
我想不起（某事）。
例 I'm afraid I can't remember his name.
我恐怕想不起他的名字。

❹ I forgot (sth.).
我忘記（某事）了。
例 I forgot why the meeting was <u>cancelled</u>.
我忘記會議為什麼取消了。

ord List

cancel [ˋkænsl] v. 取消；註銷；作廢

::::::::: 小心陷阱 :::::::::

☹ 錯誤用法：

Are you convenient to talk right now?

你現在有時間說話嗎？

☺ 正確用法：

Is it convenient for you to talk right now?

你現在有時間說話嗎？

::::::::: Biz 一點通 :::::::::

Sometimes the <u>distinction</u> between being a good <u>conversationalist</u> and being <u>intrusive</u> or annoying is quite grey. Be <u>sensitive</u> to this. Moreover, while you are trying to think of something to say to keep a conversation going, you might miss a key detail or important body language. It is extremely important to listen and let your conversation partner know you understand and value what is said. Pay close attention to non-verbal clues, such as facial expressions. If you ask someone, "Is now a good time to talk?" and see an unhappy face, that's telling you something, even if he or she says, "Sure" or "OK." In that case, it's best to keep your conversation short.

有時候擅於閒聊和冒昧或惹人厭之間的區別相當模糊。一定要敏感些。當你試著想出一些話題好讓談話繼續下去時，可能會忽略了某個關鍵細節或是重要的肢體語言。注意傾聽並讓對方知道你了解而且很重視他的談話極為重要。密切注意非言語的線索，比方說，臉部表情。如果你問某人「現在方便說話嗎？」然後看到對方滿臉不悅，這就給了你一些線索，縱使他或她嘴上說「當然」或「可以」。若是這樣，最好把談話時間縮到最短。

 ord List

distinction [dɪˋstɪŋkʃən] *n.* 區別；差別

conversationlist [kɑnvəˋseʃənˌlɪst] *n.* 喜歡說話的人；健談者

intrusive [ɪnˋtrusɪv] *adj.* 干擾的；冒昧的

sensitive [ˋsɛnsətɪv] *adj.* 敏感的；易感的

4　實戰演練 Practice Exercises

I 請為下列詞語選出最適合本章的中文譯義。

❶ keep the discussion flowing

(A) 讓討論流會　(B) 讓討論離題　(C) 讓討論順利進行

❷ Do you have a minute?

(A) 可以耽誤一點時間嗎？　(B) 你需要一分鐘的時間嗎？　(C) 可以等一下嗎？

❸ break up with someone

(A) 和某人分居　(B) 和某人一起分攤　(C) 和某人分手

II 你會如何回應下面這兩句話？

❶ Good to see you again.

(A) Thanks.

(B) Nice to see you, too.

(C) You're welcome.

❷ Are you busy now?

(A) Yes. I'm sorry.

(B) No, thank you.

(C) Yes, I have been busy lately.

III 請用下列詞語寫出一篇簡短的對話。

Tell me more.	Sorry, I've got to go.
Really?	Is now a good time to talk?
Are you sure?	I can't remember.

＊解答請見 230 頁

請求協助與回應他人請求
Asking for and Responding to Favors

Asking someone to do you a favor or responding to a request for a favor can be difficult at times, especially when the request is large or inconvenient. Yet, since, as the phrase goes, "No man is an island," favors are a common part of life both at work and in our social lives. Using appropriate phrases, such as the ones you see below, can lessen a lot of the awkwardness that is associated with requesting and responding to favors. Generally, the bigger the request, the longer and more polite the request should be.

請求別人協助或是回應別人請求協助,有時並不是件容易的事,特別是如果別人或是你必須大費周章或是會造成不便的時候。然而,正如俗話說的:「在家靠父母,出門靠朋友」,幫人忙在工作和社交場合中都是生活中常見的一部分。使用恰當的詞語,如下文你所見,可減少許多尋求協助和回應他人請求時所造成的尷尬。一般來說,你的請求愈大,就該用更多的時間以及更禮貌的態度提出。

1 Biz 必通句型 Need-to-Know Phrases

1.1 請求協助 Asking for a Favor

❶ I was wondering if...?

我在想，不知道……？

例 Mike, I was wondering if you could <u>give me a ride</u> to the airport on Friday?

邁克，我在想，不知道你星期五能不能載我去機場？

❷ Would it be OK if...?

可不可以……？

例 Would it be OK if I borrowed your notebook computer for a day or two?

我可不可以跟你借筆記型電腦用一、兩天？

❸ Is it alright if...?

能否……？

例 Is it alright if I use your camera?

我能否使用你的相機？

❹ Would you mind + V-ing ?

你介不介意……？

例 Larry, would you mind lending me some money for lunch?

賴瑞，你介不介意借我一些錢吃午餐？

 Word **L**ist

give sb. a ride 載某人一程

❺Do you think...?

你想你能……嗎？

例 Do you think you could help me move this Sunday, Norman?

你想你這個星期天能幫我搬家嗎，諾曼？

❻Would you...?

你可以……嗎？

例 Would you take care of my cat while I'm <u>on vacation</u>?

我去度假時你可以幫我照顧我的貓嗎？

❼May I...?

可以……嗎？

例 May I see your newspaper when you are finished with it?

你看完報紙之後，可以借我看嗎？

❽Can I/you...?

我／你可以……嗎？

例 Can I <u>take the day off</u> next Monday?

我下星期一可以請假嗎？

ord List

on vacation 休假；度假

take off 休假；請假

1.2 回應他人請求 Responding to Favors

同意提供協助

❶Certainly/Of course.（表示強烈接受）
當然。
例 Certainly I can give you a ride to the airport.
我當然可以載你去機場。

❷Sure, no problem.（表示強烈接受）
當然，沒問題。
例 Sure, no problem. You can pick up my notebook in the morning.
當然，沒問題。你可以早上來拿我的筆記型電腦。

❸Here you go.（把某個東西交給某人時）
拿去吧。
例 Here you go. But please take care of my camera.
拿去吧，不過請小心使用我的相機。

❹I guess so.（表示薄弱的接受）
我想應該可以。
例 I guess so. How much money do you need?
我想應該可以。你需要多少錢？

ord List

Here you go. 拿去吧。

拒絕提供協助

⑤I don't think so.（表示拒絕）

我想不行。

例 I don't think so. I'm busy on Sunday.

我想不行，我星期天有事。

⑥I'd rather not.（表示拒絕）

我還是不要吧。

例 I'd rather not. My husband hates cats.

我還是不要吧，我先生痛恨貓。

⑦I'm sorry. No.（拒絕）

對不起，不行。

例 I'm sorry. No. I want to keep the newspaper and finish it later at home.

對不起，不行，我要把報紙留著回家之後把它看完。

⑧That's not a good idea.（表示有困難）

這不是個好主意。

例 That's not a good idea. Next Monday will be a busy day, and we'll need you at work.

這不是個好主意。下星期一會很忙，我們需要你來上班。

ord List
....

would rather 寧願……（= 'd rather）

2 實戰會話 Show Time

 track 18

2.1 你可以幫我一個忙嗎？
Could You Do Me a Favor?

It seems like everybody at WHT needs some help this week. Because Darren is a very nice guy, a lot of people are asking him for favors. What should Darren do?

Paul: Hi Darren. How are you today?

Darren: Fine, thanks. How about you?

Paul: Darren, I was wondering if you could do me a bit of a favor? I'm going to Japan tomorrow and I need a ride to the airport. Would you mind driving me to the airport before work?

Darren: Sure, no problem.

Paul: Thanks a lot. Do you think you could pick me up at my house at 6:00 a.m.?

Darren: Certainly.

Paul: Thanks. That really helps me. See you tomorrow morning at six.

Sandra sees Darren and stops to talk to him.

Sandra: Hi Darren. Hey, did I tell you that my notebook has stopped working? I really need to use one while I am attending a <u>conference</u>. Would it be OK if I borrowed your notebook for a few days?

Darren: I guess so. I'll get it for you. (Darren walks over to his desk and gets his <u>portable</u> computer.) Here you go.

Sandra: Thanks a lot. I really appreciate it. I'll take good care of it.

譯 文

WHT 的每個人這週似乎都需要一些協助。由於達倫是個超級好人，許多人都請他幫忙。達倫該怎麼辦呢？

保羅：　嗨，達倫。你今天好嗎？

達倫：　很好，謝謝。你呢？

保羅：　達倫，我在想，不知道你能不能幫我一個小忙？我明天要去日本，我需要有人載我去機場。你介不介意上班前載我去機場？

達倫：　當然，沒問題。

保羅：　真是謝謝你了。你想你能不能早上六點鐘的時候到我家接我？

達倫：　當然。

保羅：　謝謝，你真是幫了我一個大忙。我們明天早上六點見。

珊德拉看見達倫，停下來和他說話。

珊德拉：嗨，達倫。嘿，我有沒有跟你說我的筆記型電腦壞了？我去參加會議時真的很需要用筆記型電腦。我可不可以跟你借筆記型電腦用幾天？

達倫：　我想應該可以。我幫妳把它拿過來。（達倫走到他的桌子那兒拿他的手提電腦。）拿去吧。

珊德拉：多謝了，我真的很感激。我會好好保管它的。

 ord List

....

conference [ˋkɑnfərəns] *n.* （正式的）會議；討論會

portable [ˋportəbl] *adj.* 可攜帶式；手提式的

2.2 拒絕提供協助 Rejecting Requests for Favors

As the day continues, Darren gets more and more requests. He starts to get tired of doing favors for everyone.

Brenda: Hi, Darren. I hate to ask you for a favor, but would you please <u>look after</u> my dog, Rusty, while I'm on vacation?

Darren: I'm sorry. No. I don't really think I have time to look after your dog Rusty, Brenda. I've got quite a few projects to finish at work.

Brenda: That's OK. Don't worry about it.

Next, Darren sees one of his coworkers, Billy Chen. Darren tries to hide, but it's too late; Billy sees him.

Billy: Darren, nice to see you again. Hey, did you know I'm moving to a new apartment this weekend? I'd like to invite you to a party next week.

Darren: Oh, great. Thanks.

Billy: May I ask you a favor?

Darren: Uhm, what?

Billy: Do you think you could help me move this Sunday?

Darren: I don't think so. I have plans to go to the beach on Sunday.

Billy: No problem. Maybe you could stop by before you go to the beach and help a little.

Darren: I'd rather not. I want to get to the beach early with my friends.

Billy: Thanks, anyway.

譯 文

隨著這一天的消逝，愈來愈多的請求向達倫湧來。他開始厭倦幫每一個人的忙。

布蘭達：嗨，達倫，我很不願意請你幫忙，但是我去度假時你可不可以幫我照料我的狗羅斯提？

達倫：　對不起，不行，我恐怕沒有時間照料妳的狗羅斯提，布蘭達。我還有公司好幾個專案要完成。

布蘭達：沒關係，別放在心上。

接著，達倫看到他的一個同事，比利‧陳。達倫試著躲起來，但為時已晚，因為比利已經看到他了。

比利：　達倫，很高興又見到你。嘿，你知不知道我這個週末要搬到一間新公寓？我想下週請你來參加派對。

達倫：　噢，好極了，謝謝。

比利：　我可以請你幫個忙嗎？

達倫：　呃，什麼忙？

比利：　你想你這個星期天可以幫我搬家嗎？

達倫：　我想不行，我星期天打算去海邊。

比利：　沒問題，也許你可以在去海邊前順道過來幫我一下。

達倫：　我想還是不要吧，我要和我的朋友早早到海邊去。

比利：　還是謝謝你。

ord List

look after 小心照料……

3 Biz 加分句型 Nice-to-Know Phrases

 track 19

3.1 謝謝幫忙你的人
Thanking Someone Who Does You a Favor

❶ **That's wonderful!**
那太好了！
例 You can help me? That's wonderful!
你可以幫我？那太好了！

❷ **Thanks a lot.**
多謝了。
例 That's great — thanks a lot.
好極了，多謝了。

❸ **I really appreciate it.**
我真的很感激。
例 I really appreciate it, Bob. Thanks.
我真的很感激，鮑伯，謝謝。

❹ **That really helps me.**
你真是幫了我一個大忙。
例 That really helps me. I owe you one.
你真是幫了我一個大忙，我欠你一份人情。

3.2 對拒絕作出回應 Responding to a Rejection

❶ No problem.
沒問題。
例 No problem — I'll ask someone else.
沒問題，我可以去問問別人。

❷ That's OK/alright.
沒關係。
例 That's OK, Frank.
沒關係，法蘭克。

❸ Don't worry about it.
別放在心上。
例 Don't worry about it, Sharon. It's not a problem.
別放在心上，莎朗，這不成問題。

❹ Thanks, anyway.
還是謝謝你。
例 Well, thanks, anyway, Randy.
嗯，還是謝謝你，藍迪。

:::::::::: 小心陷阱 ::::::::::

☹ 錯誤用法：

Would you **borrow** me some money?

你可以借我一些錢嗎？

☺ 正確用法：

Would you **lend** me some money?

你可以借我一些錢嗎？

:::::::::: Biz 一點通 ::::::::::

Be careful about asking coworkers for too many favors. You don't want to get a <u>reputation</u> as a person who is always making requests. At the same time, don't forget to show your thanks and appreciation to people who help you (perhaps offering to help them, or buying them lunch or a present if the favor is large). Also, if someone refuses to help you, make sure you don't express too much displeasure or <u>resentment</u>. After all, they <u>are under no obligation to</u> assist you, and you don't want to make enemies at work.

小心不要請同事幫太多忙。你應該不會想建立一種名聲，讓人覺得你這人總是在要求別人幫忙。同時，不要忘了對幫你忙的人表達感謝和感激（比方說，自願幫他們忙，或是，如果這個人情很大，可以請他們吃午飯或送他們禮物）。還有，如果有人拒絕幫你，要確定不要表露出太多的不悅或怨恨，畢竟，他們沒有義務要幫你，而你也不會想要在職場上樹敵。

 ord List

reputation [ˌrɛpjəˋteʃən] *n.* 名譽；名聲

resentment [rɪˋzɛntmənt] *n.* （長久累積的）怨恨、憤恨

be under an/no obligation to + V. 有／沒有義務做……

4 實戰演練 Practice Exercises

I 請為下列詞語選出最適合本章的中文譯義。

❶ Here you go.

(A) 你又來了。　(B) 拿去吧。　(C) 請往這個方向走。

❷ look after

(A) 查看　(B) 小心照料　(C) 監視

❸ be under an obligation to

(A) 無法避免……　(B) 被威脅……　(C) 有義務……

II 你會如何回應下面這兩句話？

❶ I was wondering if I could borrow your car?

(A) Thanks a lot.

(B) Because I need to use it tomorrow.

(C) I'm sorry. No.

❷ Here you go.

(A) I really appreciate it.

(B) Thanks, anyway.

(C) To work.

III 請用下列詞語寫出一篇簡短的對話。

I was wondering if	Would you mind
Sure, no problem.	Here you go.
I really appreciate it.	I don't think so.

＊解答請見 231 頁

評論好消息與壞消息
Commenting on Good and Bad News

A colleague has just told you about her car breaking down on the highway as she drove to work this morning. Or, perhaps a manager tells you his mother has passed away. What do you say? Not knowing the right words to use to respond to bad news can be awkward and make you seem socially inept. Likewise, you may be stumped at what to say when a person tells you a piece of very good news. Here are some excellent phrases that can be used when people mention good or bad news to you in the office.

一個同事剛告訴你她今天早上來上班時車子在高速公路上拋錨了；或者，或許有位經理告訴你他的母親剛過世了。你該說些什麼呢？聽到壞消息時不知該用什麼正確的字眼回應，可能會很尷尬，也會讓你顯得社交手腕很差。同樣地，當有人告訴你一個非常好的消息時，你可能也不知道要說些什麼。下面是一些很棒的詞語，當別人在辦公室裡向你提起好消息或壞消息時便可使用。

1 Biz 必通句型 Need-to-Know Phrases

1.1 評論好消息 Commenting on Good News

 track 20

❶ That's good to hear.
那真好。

例 Your son got his first job? That's good to hear.

你的兒子找到他第一份工作了？那真好。

❷ That's great/fantastic.
那好極了。

例 Our company won the project? That's fantastic.

我們公司標到那個專案了？那好極了。

❸ That's wonderful news.
真是個好消息。

例 We're getting bonuses this year? That's wonderful news.

我們今年有紅利可拿？真是個好消息。

❹ Excellent!
太好了！

例 You've been promoted to sales manager? Excellent, George!

你被升為業務經理了？太好了，喬治！

ord List

excellent [`ɛksḷ ənt] *adj.* 特優的；極好的

❺Congratulations!（常會簡化爲 "Congrats!"）

恭喜！

例 Debbie, I heard your marketing <u>campaign</u> was a success. Congratulations!

黛比，我聽說妳的行銷活動十分成功。恭喜！

❻Nice going.（用於稱讚某人的成就）

幹得好。

例 You won salesman of the month. Nice going, Judy.

妳贏得了本月最佳業務員的頭銜。幹得好，茱蒂。

❼Way to go!（用於稱讚某人的成就）

做得好！

例 Way to go, Sidney. You did a great job.

做得好，希妮。妳做得很好。

❽I knew you could do it.（表示對某人有信心）

我就知道你做得到。

例 You completed the project on time. I knew you could do it, Paul.

你準時完成了這個專案。我就知道你做得到，保羅。

 ord List

compaign [kæm`pen] *n.* 宣傳活動

1.2 評論壞消息 Commenting on Bad News

❶ That's too bad.
那真慘。
例 You lost your wallet? That's too bad, Joe.
你的皮夾弄丟了？那真慘，喬。

❷ I'm sorry to hear that.
我很遺憾聽你這麼說。
例 I'm sorry to hear that, Jenny. I hope things improve for you soon.
我很遺憾聽妳這麼說，珍妮。我希望事情很快就會好轉。

❸ That's terrible.
那太糟了。
例 Your boss <u>yelled at you</u> in front of everyone? That's terrible.
你的上司在大家面前對你大吼？那太糟了。

❹ What a shame.
真令人遺憾。
例 What a shame, Theresa. Good luck in the future.
真令人遺憾，泰瑞莎。祝妳下次好運。

Word List

yell at sb. 對某人大吼

❺ What a pity.

真可惜。

例 You weren't able to get that new job? What a pity.

你沒能獲得那份新工作？真可惜。

❻ That must have been quite a shock to you.（某件非常嚴重的事發生時）

你一定很震驚。

例 You got fired? That must have been quite a shock to you.

你被開除了？你一定很震驚。

❼ Are you OK?（某件非常嚴重的事發生或某人受傷時）

你還好吧？

例 Your husband has <u>cancer</u>? Are you OK?

妳丈夫得了癌症？妳還好吧？

❽ My <u>condolences</u>.（有人死亡時）

謹致上我的哀悼之意。

例 I'm very sorry to hear your mother died. My condolences.

聽到你母親過世的消息我很難過。謹致上我的哀悼之意。

 ord List

cancer [ˈkænsə] *n.* 癌症；惡性腫瘤

condolence [kənˈdoləns] *n.* 弔唁；哀悼

2 實戰會話 Show Time

2.1 首先，好消息 First, the Good News

 track 21

It's a day filled with a lot of good news at WHT. Paul has been promoted to sales manager,and the marketing department has received an award from a marketing magazine for one of its marketing campaigns.

Darren: Paul, I heard you were promoted to sales manager.

Paul: That's right. I just found out yesterday.

Darren: That's good news. Congratulations!

Paul: Thanks a lot, Darren.

Brenda comes out of the copy room holding a file folder.

Paul: Hi, Brenda. Did you hear I got promoted yesterday to sales manager?

Brenda: Really? Excellent. Nice going!

Paul: Thanks. I'm having a party to celebrate at my house on Saturday night. Would you like to come?

Brenda: Well, I'm feeling a little depressed about not getting into graduate school. I'm not sure I'd be much fun.

Paul: <u>There's no use crying over spilled milk</u>. I'm sure you'll get into another school later.

Brenda: I guess you're right. OK, I'll come to your party.

At that moment, Shirley Saunders — the head of WHT's marketing department — walks by.

Darren: Hi, Shirley. I read in this month's company <u>newsletter</u> that the marketing department won an award.

Shirley: Yes, we did, Darren. The award was from *Marketing Today*, a large international trade magazine. It should give us a lot of good <u>publicity</u>.

Darren: That's wonderful news.

WHT 今天充滿了好消息。保羅被升為業務經理，而行銷部門的一個行銷活動獲得一本行銷雜誌頒發的一個獎項。

達倫：　保羅，我聽說你被升為業務經理了。

保羅：　沒錯，我昨天才知道的。

達倫：　真是個好消息。恭喜！

保羅：　多謝，達倫。

布蘭達從影印間走出來，手上拿著一個檔案夾。

保羅：　嗨，布蘭達。妳有沒有聽說我昨天被升為業務經理？

布蘭達：真的啊？太好了。幹得好！

保羅：　謝謝。我星期六晚上要在我家舉辦一場派對慶祝一下。妳要不要來？

布蘭達：嗯，我沒有申請到研究所覺得有些沮喪。我不知道會不會掃大家的興。

保羅：　覆水難收，不過我確定妳之後一定能申請到其他的研究所。

布蘭達：我想你說得對。好吧，我會參加你的派對。

此時，WHT 行銷部門主管雪莉‧桑德斯正好路過。

達倫：　嗨，雪莉，我看到這個月的公司業務通訊上說行銷部贏得了一個獎。

雪莉：　是的，我們贏得了一個獎，達倫。那個獎項是一本大型國際企業界雜誌《今日行銷》所頒發的。應該會帶給我們不少正面的宣傳。

達倫：　真是個好消息。

There's no use crying over spilled milk. 覆水難收。
newsletter [`njuz͵lɛtə] *n.* （公司、機關的）簡訊；業務通訊
publicity [pʌb`lɪsətɪ] *n.* 宣傳；廣告 (give ~ to...)

2.2 現在，壞消息 Now, the Bad News

After that day filled with good news, the next day brings a bit of bad news. A new employee named Tommy Kuo failed to pass the <u>probationary</u> period at WHT.

Sandra: Darren, do you remember that guy who started at WHT about the same time as you did? I think his name is Tommy.

Darren: Yeah, he was in the same training class as us. What about him?

Sandra: He didn't pass his probation. They let him go.

Darren: That's too bad. I <u>kind of</u> liked him.

<u>Speak of the devil</u>, Tommy walks by, head down, carrying a box of his personal <u>effects</u>.

Sandra: Hi Tommy. I'm sorry to hear that you're leaving us.

Darren: Yes, that must have been quite a shock to you. So, what are you going to do now?

Tommy looks up with a <u>pitiful</u> expression, as if he<u>'s about to</u> cry.

Tommy: Well I, I mean...

Darren: Please forgive me, Tommy. That was <u>inconsiderate</u> of me. You probably don't have any <u>firm</u> plans right now.

Tommy: No...not really. I'm pretty upset about things right now.

Sandra: I know it must be really tough right now, Tommy, but tomorrow's another day. I'm sure you'll feel a bit better about things tomorrow or the next day. Anyway, good luck to you in the future.

Darren: Yes, time heals all <u>wounds</u>. Take care, Tommy.

Tommy: Thanks, Sandra, Darren. I... I really appreciate it.

在那天到處傳來好消息之後，第二天卻傳出一些壞消息。一個 WHT 的新員工湯米·郭沒有通過試用期。

珊德拉：達倫，你記不記得大約和你同期進 WHT 的那個男生？我想他叫湯米。

達倫：　記得，他和我們上同一期的訓練課程。他怎麼了？

珊德拉：他試用期沒過。他們叫他走路。

達倫：　那真慘。我還滿喜歡他的。

說曹操，曹操到。湯米垂頭喪氣地走過來，手上拿著一箱他的私人物品。

珊德拉：嗨，湯米。很遺憾聽到你要離開公司。

達倫：　是啊，你一定感到很震驚。那，你現在打算怎麼做？

湯米一臉悲慘地抬起頭來，像是快要哭出來的樣子。

湯米：　嗯，我想……

達倫：　請原諒我，湯米。我真是太不顧慮你的感受了。你此刻可能還沒有任何具體的計畫。

湯米：　是……是沒有。我現在心情滿糟的。

珊德拉：我知道你現在一定很不好受，湯米，但是明天又是全新的一天，我確定你明天或後天一定會覺得好一些。無論如何，祝你以後一切順利。

達倫：　是啊，時間可以治癒一切。保重了，湯米。

湯米：　謝了，珊德拉、達倫。我……我真的很感激。

ord List

probationary [prə`beʃən‚ɛrɪ] *adj.* 試用的；實習中的（probation [prə`beʃən] *n.* 試用期）

kind of + adj./V.【口語】有幾分；有一點

speak of the devil　說曹操，曹操就到

effect [ɪ`fɛkt] *n.* 動產（personal effects 隨身物品；家當）

pitiful [`pɪtɪfəl] *adj.* 令人同情的；悲慘的

be about to 即將（做）……

inconsiderate [‚ɪnkən`sɪdərɪt] *adj.* 不體諒（別人）的

firm [fɜm] *adj.* 堅定的；斷然的

wound [wund] *n.* 創傷；傷害

3 Biz 加分句型 Nice-to-Know Phrases

 track 22

3.1 為你作的評論道歉
Apologizing for a Comment You Made

❶ Please forgive me (for sth.).
請原諒我（某件事）。
例 Please forgive me for saying that.
請原諒我那麼說。

❷ That was inconsiderate of me.
我真是太不顧慮你的感受了。
例 That was inconsiderate of me — I apologize.
我真是太不顧慮你的感受了，我道歉。

❸ Excuse me for <u>intruding</u>.
請原諒我太冒昧了。
例 Excuse me for intruding. I shouldn't have asked that.
請原諒我太冒昧了。我不該問的。

❹ I'm sorry. I didn't mean to <u>pry into (sth.)</u>.
對不起，我無意刺探（某件事）。
例 I'm sorry, I didn't mean to pry into your personal life.
對不起，我無意刺探你的私生活。

 Word List

intrude [ɪn`trud] *v.* 干涉；干擾（他人的事）
pry into sth. 窺伺……；刺探……

(3.2) 評論壞消息的恰當成語
Appropriate Idioms for Commenting on Bad News

❶ There's no use crying over spilled milk.

覆水難收。

例 There's no use crying over spilled milk. You can't do anything about it now.

覆水難收，你現在也無能為力了。

❷ What's done is done.

木已成舟。

例 What's done is done, Trudy. You <u>might as well</u> accept it.

木已成舟，楚蒂，妳還是接受它吧。

❸ Tomorrow's another day.

明天又是全新的一天。

例 Tomorrow's another day. Things will seem better tomorrow.

明天又是全新的一天。明天事情會好轉的。

❹ Time heals all wounds.

時間可以治癒一切。

例 I know it's difficult right now, but time heals all wounds.

我知道你現在很難受，但是時間可以治癒一切。

ord List

might as well 還是⋯⋯；（與其⋯⋯）還不如⋯⋯

======== 小心陷阱 ========

☹ 錯誤用法：
Brian was promoted **as** manager.
布萊恩被升為經理。

☺ 正確用法：
Brian was promoted **to** manager.
OR
Brian was promoted manager.
布萊恩被升為經理。

======== Biz 一點通 ========

It's always easier to comment on good news than bad news. Saying too much or asking difficult and/or personal questions about the piece of bad news you've just heard could make things even more <u>awkward</u>. As a rule, make sure to check the person's facial expressions and other body language to help you <u>estimate</u> how difficult it is for the person to talk about the bad news. Generally, the more difficult it appears for them to talk, the less you should say. Likewise, while <u>proverbs</u> can be good to use and sound <u>sympathetic</u>, don't overuse them or you run the risk of sounding <u>insincere</u>.

評論好消息總是比評論壞消息簡單得多。說太多或是針對這個你剛聽來的壞消息問一些很難回答和／或私人的問題，可能會讓事情變得更尷尬。一個基本原則就是，務必對這個人察言觀色並觀察其肢體語言，將有助於你評估對方談論這個壞消息有多困難。一般來說，如果討論起來感覺愈困難，你就應該說愈少的話。同樣地，諺語雖然可能很好用，聽起來又十分富有同情心，但別過度使用，不然你就有可能會聽起來假惺惺的。

 ord List

awkward [ˈɔkwəd] *adj.* 難為情的；不自在的
estimate [ˈɛstəmet] *v.* 評估；推斷
proverb [ˈprɑvɝb] *n.* 諺語；格言

sympathetic [ˌsɪmpəˈθɛtɪk] *adj.* 同情的
insincere [ˌɪnsɪnˈsɪr] *adj.* 不誠實的；虛偽的

4　實戰演練 Practice Exercises

I 請為下列詞語選出最適合本章的中文譯義。

❶ I kind of like him.

(A) 我是他喜歡的類型。　(B) 我還蠻喜歡他的。　(C) 我跟他有點像。

❷ What a shame.

(A) 真丟臉。　(B) 真抱歉。　(C) 真令人遺憾。

❸ My condolences.

(A) 我的不幸。　(B) 我很難過。　(C) 謹致上我的哀悼之意。

II 你會如何回應下面這兩句話？

❶ Nice going.

(A) To my home.

(B) I feel fine, thanks.

(C) Thanks.

❷ I just got fired!

(A) Congrats!

(B) Are you OK?

(C) There's no use crying over spilled milk.

III 請用下列詞語寫出一篇簡短的對話。

That's great.　　　　Way to go!

I'm sorry to hear that.　What a shame.

Please forgive me.　　Tomorrow's another day.

＊解答請見 232 頁

第 **8** 章

商務電話用語
Business over the Phone

Speaking on the telephone in English can present a few challenges for the non-native speaker. On the phone, there are no facial clues or gestures to help the listener. This means that you have to concentrate harder, and it also means that you must make sure to use proper terminology so the other person clearly understands you. Here are some very specific phrases used for talking on the telephone in English.

用英文講電話對母語非英語的人來說，可能會是項挑戰。在電話上，聽電話的人無法借助對方的面部表情或手勢，這意味你必須更加專心地聽，也表示你必須確定自己使用正確的詞語，這樣對方才能清楚了解你的意思。下面是一些用英語講電話時的特殊用語。

Biz 必通句型 Need-to-Know Phrases

1.1 打電話與接電話
Making and Answering Calls

打電話

❶ May I speak to (name)?
能不能請（姓名）接電話？
例 Good morning. May I speak to Bob?
早安。能不能請鮑伯接電話？

❷ Is (name) in?
（姓名）在嗎？
例 Hello. Is Roberta in right now?
喂，蘿波塔現在在嗎？

❸ I'm looking for (name).
我找（姓名）。
例 Hi, I'm looking for Brenda.
嗨，我找布蘭達。

❹ Is this (name)?（不確定接電話者是否為正確的人或公司時）
請問是（名稱）嗎？
例 Hello. Is this the ABC Computer Company?
喂，請問是 ABC 電腦公司嗎？

接電話

❺Hello, this is (name).（向來電者表明身分）
喂，我是（姓名）。
例 Hello, this is Lily speaking.
喂，我是莉莉。

❻Speaking.（當某人要找的人正是你時）
我就是。
例 Speaking. How can I help you?
我就是。我能幫你什麼忙嗎？

❼May I ask who's calling?（當來電者未自我介紹時）
請問您是哪位？
例 Pardon me. May I ask who's calling?
對不起，請問您是哪位？

❽Who's speaking, please?（當來電者未自我介紹時）
請問哪位？
例 Excuse me. Who's speaking, please?
對不起，請問哪位？

1.2 轉接電話和記錄留言
Transferring Calls and Taking Messages

轉接電話

❶Do you know the <u>extension</u> number?（詢問某一分機號碼）
你知道分機號碼嗎？
例 Do you know the extension number for Mr. Saunders?
你知道桑德斯先生的分機號碼嗎？

❷I'll <u>transfer</u> you.
我幫你轉接。
例 I'll transfer you right away.
我馬上幫你轉接。

❸I'll <u>put you through</u>.
我幫你轉過去。
例 I'll put you through to Jane now.
我現在就幫你轉過去給珍。

❹One moment please.
請稍候。
例 One moment please, Mr. Smith.
請稍候，史密斯先生。

ord List

extension [ɪk`stɛnʃən] *n.*（電話的）分機；內線
transfer [træns`fɜ] *v.* 轉接
put sb. through 幫（某人）接通……；轉接（電話）

對方當下無法接聽電話時

❺ The line is busy.

電話忙線中。

例 I'm sorry. The line is busy.

對不起，電話忙線中。

❻ (Name) is on another line.

（姓名）在另一線上。

例 I'm sorry. David is on another line right now.

對不起，大衛現在正在另一線上。

❼ Would you like to <u>hold</u>?（詢問來電者是否要等待）

您要在線上等嗎？

例 Would you like to hold for Ms. Jones?

您要在線上等瓊斯小姐嗎？

❽ Would you like to call back later?

您要不要稍後再打過來？

例 Would you like to call back later this afternoon?

您要不要今天下午再打過來？

ord List

....

hold [hold] *v.* 在電話上稍等

2 實戰會話 Show Time

2.1 致電多倫多辦公室 Calling the Toronto Office

In order to answer some questions about the designs for the German project, Darren is calling WHT's consultant in Toronto, who helps WHT deal with international client. Brenda, the consultant based in Taipei, is <u>currently</u> on vacation.

Darren:	Hello, my name is Darren Jiang. I'm calling from WHT in Taipei. May I speak to Freda Waterston please?
Receptionist:	Do you know the extension number for Ms. Waterston?
Darren:	No, I'm sorry. I don't.
Receptionist:	That's OK. Let me check. Yes, her extension number is 316. One moment please. I'll put you through.
Darren:	Thank you.
Bob:	Good morning. This is Bob Jenkins.
Darren:	Oh, hello. I'm looking for Freda Waterston.
Bob:	I'm sorry. You've got the wrong number. Her extension number is 361, not 316. I'll transfer you.

Darren's call is transferred.

Darren:	Hello, is this Freda Waterston?
Freda:	Yes, speaking.
Darren:	Ms. Waterston, I was wondering if you could answer a few questions about a project I'm working on.
Freda:	May I ask who's calling?
Darren:	Sorry, this is Darren Jiang from WHT in Taipei.
Freda:	Hi Darren. What can I do for you?

文

為了回答一些關於德國專案設計圖的疑問，達倫正在打電話給 WHT 駐多倫多負責協助與國際客戶往來的顧問。派駐台北的顧問布蘭達目前正在休假。

達倫：　喂，我是達倫‧江。我從 WHT 台北辦事處打來。能不能麻煩請佛瑞達‧瓦特森接電話？

櫃檯：　你知道瓦特森小姐的分機號碼嗎？

達倫：　抱歉，我不知道。

櫃檯：　沒關係。讓我查一下。是的，她的分機號碼是 316。請稍候，我幫你轉過去。

達倫：　謝謝。

鮑伯：　早安，我是鮑伯‧詹金斯。

達倫：　噢，你好。我找佛瑞達‧瓦特森。

鮑伯：　抱歉，你撥錯號碼了。她的分機是 361，不是 316。我幫你轉。

達倫的電話被轉接過去。

達倫：　喂，請問是佛瑞達‧瓦特森嗎？

佛瑞達：是，我就是。

達倫：　瓦特森小姐，我在想，不知道妳能不能回答我幾個關於我現在正在做的一項專案的問題。

佛瑞達：請問您是哪位？

達倫：　抱歉，我是 WHT 台北辦事處的達倫‧江。

佛瑞達：嗨，達倫。我能幫你什麼忙？

Word List
....

currently [ˈkɝəntlɪ] *adv.* 目前；現在

2.2 打電話到德國 A Call to Germany

Now that the Toronto office has answered Darren's questions, he needs to check a few things with <u>officials</u> in Germany concerning the project.

Receptionist: Hello, this is the planning department.

Darren: Hello. Is Mr. Schneider in?

Receptionist: Yes. I'll transfer you.

Darren: Thank you.

While Darren is on hold, he checks his <u>stock options</u> on the WHT website.

Receptionist: I'm sorry. The line is busy. Would you like to hold?

Darren: OK.

While waiting, it occurs to Darren that he should use <u>Skype</u> for his next international call.

Receptionist: I'm sorry. Mr. Schneider is still on another line. Would you like to leave a message or would you like to call back later?

Darren: I'd like to leave him a message. Could you tell him that Darren Jiang from WHT in Taipei called? Please ask him to call me at my office. He has my number.

Receptionist: Certainly, Mr. Jiang. Goodbye.

Darren: Goodbye.

Later in the day, Mr. Schneider returns Darren's call.

Darren: Hello, this is Darren speaking.

Schneider: Hello Darren, this is Heinz Schneider.

Darren: Hi Mr. Schneider. Thank you for returning my call. I have a few questions I want to...

Schneider: Excuse me. The line isn't clear.

Darren: I said I have a few questions to ask you...

Schneider: What was that? Could you <u>speak up</u> a little?

Darren: I think there's a problem with your line. I will call you back in a minute.

文

在多倫多辦公室回答了達倫的問題之後，他現在需要和德國官員確認與這項專案相關的幾件事。

總機：　喂，這裡是規劃部。

達倫：　喂，史奈德先生在嗎？

總機：　在，我幫您轉接。

達倫：　謝謝。

達倫在線上等待的同時，他到 WHT 網站上查看了一下他的股票選擇權。

總機：　對不起，電話忙線中。您要在線上等嗎？

達倫：　好的。

在等的時候，達倫想到下一次他應該用 Skype 打國際電話。

總機：　抱歉，史奈德先生還在另一線上。您要留言或是稍後再打過來？

達倫：　我想留言給他。能不能請你告訴他 WHT 台北辦事處的達倫‧江打過電話給他？麻煩請他打到我的辦公室來。他有我的電話。

總機：　沒問題，江先生。再見。

達倫：　再見。

當天稍晚，史奈德先生回達倫的電話。

達倫：　喂，我是達倫。

史奈德：喂，達倫，我是漢斯‧史奈德。

達倫：　嗨，史奈德先生，謝謝你回我的電話。我有幾個問題想要……

史奈德：抱歉，線路不太清楚。

達倫：　我說我有幾個問題要問你……

史奈德：你說什麼？你能說大聲一點嗎？

達倫：　我想你的線路有問題。我稍後再打回去給你。

ord List

official [ə`fɪʃəl] *n.* 公務員；官員

stock option [`stɑk `ɑpʃən] *n.* 股票選擇權；認股權

Skype [skaɪp] *n.* 一種須透過網路使用的即時通訊程式，可在全球進行高品質免費語音通訊。

speak up 更大聲地說

3 Biz 加分句型 Nice-to-Know Phrases

track 25

3.1 記錄與留下留言
Taking and Leaving Messages

記錄留言

❶ Would you like to leave a message?
您要不要留言？
例 Would you like to leave a message for Brent?
你要不要留言給布藍特？

❷ May I take a message for him/her?
我可以幫你記下留言給他／她嗎？
例 She's not in. May I take a message for her?
她不在。我可以幫你記下留言給她嗎？

留下留言

❸ Could you tell him/her (sth.)?
能不能麻煩你告訴他／她（某件事）？
例 Could you tell him that the meeting is at 3 p.m. tomorrow?
能不能麻煩你告訴他會議是明天下午三點？

❹ Please ask him/her (to do sth.).
麻煩請他／她（做某件事）。
例 Please ask her to call me when she gets in.
麻煩請她進來後打電話給我。

3.2 處理問題 Dealing with Problems

❶ You've got the wrong number.
你撥錯號碼了。
例 I'm sorry. You've got the wrong number.
對不起，你撥錯號碼了。

❷ There's no such person here.
這裡沒有這個人。
例 Betty Chou? No, there's no such person here.
貝蒂·周？沒有，這裡沒有這個人。

❸ The line isn't clear.
線路不太清楚。
例 I can't hear you — the line isn't clear.
我聽不到你在說什麼，線路不太清楚。

❹ Could you speak up?
您能說大聲一點嗎？
例 Pardon me. Could you speak up, please?
對不起，您能說大聲一點嗎？

:::::::::: 小心陷阱 ::::::::::

☹ 錯誤用法：

There's a problem **on** the line.

線路有問題。

☺ 正確用法：

There's a problem **with** the line.

線路有問題。

:::::::::: Biz 一點通 ::::::::::

Just as politeness is important in <u>face-to-face</u> conversation, it is equally or even more important to use it on the telephone, since there are no facial expressions or <u>gestures</u> to give the other person clues as to how you are feeling or what you mean. Saying things like "please" and "thank you" are important for making a good impression. Even when you call a wrong number, you should say "Sorry," or "Sorry to bother you." You may feel <u>embarrassed</u> about dialing a wrong number, but it is considered <u>extremely</u> rude to simply hang up without saying anything.

正如禮貌在面對面交談中非常重要，在電話上保持禮貌的重要性更是有過之而無不及，因為對方無法透過面部表情或手勢來揣測你的感受或意思。要建立起良好的印象，說「請」和「謝謝」之類的話相當重要。就連撥錯號碼時，也應該要說聲「對不起」或者是「抱歉打擾你了」。撥錯號碼可能會讓你覺得不好意思，但是一句話都不說就把電話掛上會被認為極度地無禮。

Ｗord List

face-to-face *adj.* 面對面的

gesture [ˋdʒɛstʃɚ] *n.* 手勢；動作；表情

embarrassed [ɪmˋbærəst] *adj.* 困窘的；尷尬的

extremely [ikˋstrimlɪ] *adv.* 極端地；極度地

4 實戰演練 Practice Exercises

Ⅰ 請為下列詞語選出最適合本章的中文譯義。

❶ take a message

(A) 拿走訊息　(B) 將留言帶著走　(C) 記下留言

❷ I'll put you through.

(A) 我幫你轉接。　(B) 我會陪你度過。　(C) 我會讓你過關。

❸ Would you like to hold?

(A) 您想舉辦嗎？　(B) 您要在線上等嗎？　(C) 您想撐下去嗎？

Ⅱ 你會如何回應下面這兩句話？

❶ Who's speaking, please?

(A) This is Steven.

(B) I, Steven.

(C) Speaking.

❷ I'm sorry, the line is busy.

(A) I'll transfer you.

(B) That's OK. I'll hold.

(C) No, I'm not busy now.

Ⅲ 請用下列詞語寫出一篇簡短的對話。

May I speak to	May I ask who's calling?
I'll put you through.	Would you like to leave a message?
The line is busy.	Please ask him/her

＊解答請見 233 頁

第 **9** 章

談論器材設備問題
Talking About Equipment Problems

Dealing with equipment problems is a part of the daily routine at the office. If you can fix the problem yourself, then there may be no need to communicate the problem to anyone else. However, often we can't repair the malfunction ourselves and we have to rely on others. When you're up against a piece of office equipment that won't cooperate, knowing the proper vocabulary and phrasing are both key in executing the repair.

處理器材設備問題是辦公室例行公事的一部分。如果你自己可以解決這個問題，也許就不需要把這個問題傳達給別人知道。然而我們通常都無法自行修理故障的器材，而必須依靠他人。當你得面對一件不願配合的辦公室器材時，在處理過程中知道恰當的辭彙與措辭十分重要。

Biz 必通句型 Need-to-Know Phrases

1.1 處理設備問題（1）
Dealing with Equipment Problems I

描述某樣器材無法正常運作或故障

❶ There's a problem with (sth.)
（某東西）有問題。
例 There's a problem with my computer.
我的電腦有問題。

❷ Something is wrong with (sth.)
（某東西）有些不太對勁。
例 Excuse me, something is wrong with the fax machine.
對不起，傳真機有些不太對勁。

❸ We need to replace (sth.)
我們需要把（某東西）換掉。
例 We need to replace the toner cartridge in the printer.
我們需要更換印表機裡的墨水匣。

❹ (Sth.) is not working.
（某東西）不靈光。
例 My mouse is not working.
我的滑鼠不靈光。

 Word List

replace [rɪˋples] v. 替換；更換
toner cartridge [ˋtonəˏ ˏkɑrtrɪdʒ] n. 墨水匣

❺ (Sth.) is broken. / (Sth.) has broken down.
（某東西）故障了。
例 The <u>photocopier</u> is broken.
影印機故障了。

❻ (Sth.) is out of order.
（某東西）壞了。
例 My telephone is <u>out of order</u>.
我的電話壞了。

❼ (Sth.) needs fixing.
（某東西）需要修理。
例 The air conditioner needs fixing.
冷氣機需要修理。

❽ (Sth.) has <u>conked out</u>.
（某東西）突然故障了。
例 The <u>scanner</u> has conked out.
掃瞄器突然故障了。

Ⓦord List

photocopier [ˋfotəˋkɑpɪɚ] *n.* 影印機
out of order 故障
conk out【俚】（機器等）失靈；突然發生故障
scanner [ˋskænɚ] *n.* 掃瞄器

115

1.2 處理設備問題（2）
Dealing with Equipment Problems II

描述某樣設備並未完全故障但有問題

❶ (Sth.) is not responding.
（某東西）沒有回應。
例 The Internet connection is not responding.
網際網路連線沒有回應。

❷ (Sth.) is acting up.
（某東西）出了毛病。
例 Did you know the projector is acting up?
你知不知道投影機出了毛病？

❸ (Sth.) is jammed.
（某東西）卡住了。
例 The printer is jammed again.
印表機又卡紙了。

❹ (Sth.) is stuck.
（某東西）卡住了。
例 The photocopier is stuck.
影印機卡住了。

Word List
act up（機器等）出毛病
projector [prə`dʒɛktə] *n.* 投影機
jam [dʒæm] *v.* （機器等）卡住
stuck [stʌk] *adj.* 卡住不能動彈的

描述某樣東西不足

❺We need more (sth.)

我們需要更多（某物）。

例 We need more batteries.

我們需要更多電池。

❻We're <u>short of</u> (sth.)

我們（某物）短缺。

例 We're short of paper.

我們紙張短缺。

❼(Sth.) has <u>run out of</u> (sth.)

（某物）的（某物）用完了。

例 The printer has run out of ink.

印表機的墨水用完了。

❽There's no more (sth.)

沒有（某物）了。

例 There's no more coffee.

沒有咖啡了。

ord List

short of sth. 短缺（某物）

run out of sth. 用完（某物）

2 實戰會話 Show Time

2.1 技術挑戰 Technological Challenges

 track 27

As the deadline for the designs for the German project gets closer, Darren is working hard and trying to complete the project on time. This day, however, is one filled with equipment problems and <u>frustration</u> for Darren.

Darren: Excuse me, Sandra. Something is wrong with the photocopier. I tried to make a few copies and all I get now is a <u>blinking</u> red light.

Sandra: Let me take a look. Oh, I see the problem — it's jammed.

Sandra pulls out the jammed paper and closes the <u>access panel</u>.

Sandra: There, it's OK now.

Darren: Thanks a lot.

After making some copies, Darren needs to fax them to Germany.

Darren: Oh no! The fax machine is not working!

Steve: Is it out of order again? We need to replace that machine because it always needs fixing. Why don't you just scan the documents into your computer and then fax them from your computer?

Darren: Great idea! Thanks, Steve.

Darren tries to use his computer to fax the documents, but he keeps getting an error message.

Darren: <u>Darn</u>! I can't make it work. Sandra, sorry to bother you, but do you know how this fax software works? I'm not familiar with it. I have a different program on my home computer.

> Sandra: Sorry, Darren. My monitor has conked out. I haven't got time right now.

譯文

隨著那項德國專案設計圖的最後期限逐漸逼近，達倫埋頭苦幹，試著要準時完成專案。然而，這一天對達倫來說卻是充滿器材問題和挫敗的日子。

達倫：　對不起，珊德拉，影印機不太對勁。我試著要影印一些東西，但是眼前只見一個紅燈在不斷閃爍。

珊德拉：讓我看看。喔，我知道問題之所在，它卡紙了。

珊德拉把卡紙拉出來，然後把檢修門關起來。

珊德拉：哪，現在可以了。

達倫：　真是謝謝妳了。

在印完幾張東西後，達倫需要把它們傳真到德國去。

達倫：　噢不！傳真機不靈光！

史提夫：又壞了嗎？我們需要把那台機器換掉，它老需要修理。你何不乾脆把文件掃瞄到你的電腦裡，然後再從你的電腦把它們傳真出去？

達倫：　好主意！謝了，史提夫。

達倫試著要用他的電腦傳真文件，但是他一直得到操作錯誤的訊號。

達倫：　可惡！怎麼試都不成功。珊德拉，抱歉來煩妳，妳知不知道這個傳真軟體怎麼用？我對它不太熟，我家裡的電腦上是另一種程式。

珊德拉：對不起，達倫，我的螢幕突然故障，我現在沒有空。

Word List

frustration [frʌ`streʃən] *n.* 挫折；失敗
blink [blɪŋk] *v.* 閃爍
access panel [`æksɛs ˏpæn]] *n.* 檢修門（panel *n.* 儀表盤）
darn [dɑrn] *v.* 該死；糟了（= damn 的委婉說法）

2.2 愈滾愈大的技術問題 Snowballing Tech Problems

Without Sandra's assistance, Darren finally figures out how to operate the fax software correctly. Unfortunately, there are more problems <u>lurking</u> for him.

Darren: Wait a minute. What's going on? Now there's a problem with my computer!

Darren grabs the <u>receiver</u> and calls the IT department.

Darren: Hello, this is Darren on 11. My computer is acting up. It's not working properly.

IT: OK, I'll come right up and take a look.

Darren: Great, thanks.

The moment the IT guy arrives, Darren's computer makes a loud noise and starts smoking.

IT: Well, I think your computer is a <u>write-off</u>. It can't be fixed. I have a notebook computer here you can use until we get you a <u>replacement</u> for your <u>desktop</u> computer.

Darren: OK, thanks. Hey, this notebook is broken too. It won't <u>boot</u>!

IT: Let me take a look. No, it's not. The battery has run out of power. Just use the <u>power cord</u> for now. We're short of batteries right now, so I can't give you a new one.

Darren: No problem. Could you show me how to use some of the software programs for making presentations?

IT: Sure. Let's start by clicking this icon here.

雖然沒有珊德拉的幫助，達倫最後還是搞懂了要如何正確操作那個傳真軟體。
不幸的是，還有更多的問題在等著他。

達倫：　等一下，這是怎麼回事？現在換我的電腦有問題了！

達倫抓起話筒，打到資訊部。

達倫：　喂，我是十一樓的達倫。我的電腦出毛病了，它無法正常運作。

資訊部：好，我馬上上去幫你看一下。

達倫：　太好了，謝謝。

當資訊部的人到的時候，達倫的電腦發出一個很大的聲響，然後開始冒煙。

資訊部：呃，我想你的電腦是報銷了；它是修不好了。在我們幫你弄來一台替
　　　　換你這台桌上型電腦前，我這兒有一台筆記型電腦你可以先用。

達倫：　好，謝謝。嘿，這台筆記型電腦也故障了；它沒辦法開機！

資訊部：讓我看看。沒有，它沒壞，是電池的電用完了。暫時先用電源線吧。
　　　　我們目前沒有電池了，所以我沒辦法給你一個新的。

達倫：　不要緊。你能不能教我如何使用一些製作簡報的軟體程式？

資訊部：當然可以。我們就從按下這邊這個圖示開始吧。

Word List

snowball [ˋsnoˌbɔl] *v.* 使……像滾雪球般逐漸增大
lurk [lɝk] *v.* 躲藏；埋伏；潛伏
receiver [rɪˋsivə] *n.* （電話的）話筒
write-off [ˋraɪtˌɔf] *n.* 報廢的東西；失敗的人
replacement [rɪˋplesmənt] *n.* 替代物
desktop [ˋdɛskˌtɑp] *n.* 桌上型電腦
boot [but] *v.* 【電腦】開機；啟動程式
power cord [ˋpauəˌkɔrd] *n.* 電源線（cord *n.* 絕緣電線）

3 Biz 加分句型 Nice-to-Know Phrases

3.1 尋求協助 Seeking Help

track 28

請求協助

❶ Do you know how (to do sth.)?
你知不知道如何（做某件事）？
例 Do you know how to use this machine?
你知不知道如何使用這台機器？

❷ Could you show me (how to do sth.)?
你能不能教我如何（做某件事）？
例 Could you show me how to use this?
你能不能教我如何使用這個？

表達你不知道如何做某件事

❸ I'm not sure how (to do sth.).
我不確定要如何（做某件事）。
例 I'm not sure how to send a fax with this machine.
我不確定要如何用這台機器傳真。

❹ I'm not familiar with (sth.).
我不太熟悉（某東西）。
例 I'm not familiar with this software program.
我不太熟悉這個軟體程式。

3.2 描述無法修復的機器
Describing Machines That Can't Be Fixed

❶ **(Sth.) is <u>wrecked</u>.**
（某東西）壞了。
例 This monitor is wrecked. There was a power <u>surge</u>.
這個螢幕壞了。剛才電源陡增。

❷ **(Sth.) is ruined.**
（某東西）毀了。
例 The scanner is ruined. Karen spilled coffee on it.
掃瞄器毀了。凱倫把咖啡灑在上面。

❸ **(Sth.) can't be fixed.**
（某東西）是修不好了。
例 Bad news. The notebook can't be fixed.
壞消息。這台筆記型電腦是修不好了。

❹ **(Sth.) is a write-off.**
（某東西）報銷了。
例 The fax machine is a write-off. Get a new one.
傳真機報銷了。買台新的吧。

ord List

wrecked [ˋrɛkt] *adj.* 毀壞的
surge [sɝdʒ] *n.* 浪湧；陡增

☹ 錯誤用法：

The printer is **wrong**.

印表機壞了無法運作。

☺ 正確用法：

The printer is **not working**.

印表機壞了無法運作。

::::::::: Biz 一點通 :::::::::

When <u>encountering</u> an equipment problem, it's <u>tempting</u> to ask the first person you see to help you repair it. However, that person may not know how to fix the problem either, so it's probably a good idea to ask "Do you know how to fix this?" or "Do you know who can fix this?" rather than immediately saying, "Hey, give me a hand fixing this." But whatever you do, the next time something <u>breaks down</u> at work, try describing the problem with the phases from this chapter.

在碰到器材問題時，你會很自然地想請你碰到的第一個人幫你修理，但是那個人可能也不知道要怎麼解決這個問題，因此你可能最好先問：「你知道要怎麼修理這個嗎？」或「你知道誰能修理這個嗎？」，而不要直接說：「嘿，幫我修理這個。」不過，不管你怎麼做，下次在工作時如果有東西壞掉，試著用本章的詞語來描述問題。

 Word **List**

encounter [ɪn`kauntɚ] *v.* 遭遇（問題、危險等）；碰見（人）

tempting [`tɛmptɪŋ] *adj.* 引人心動；誘人的

break down （機器等）損壞；發生故障

實戰演練 Practice Exercises

I 請為下列詞語選出最適合本章的中文譯義。

❶ conk out

(A) 毆打 (B) 突然故障 (C) 取消

❷ act up

(A)出毛病 (B) 代表 (C) 採取行動

❸ write-off

(A) 交稿 (B) 背書 (C) 報銷的東西

II 你會如何回應下面這兩句話？

❶ We've run out of paper.

(A) I'll get some more.

(B) Where to?

(C) It's ruined.

❷ The printer is a write-off.

(A) Could you show me how to use it?

(B) I'm not familiar with it.

(C) We should replace it.

III 請用下列詞語寫出一篇簡短的對話。

something is wrong with   needs fixing

is broken   run out of

wrecked   could you show me

＊解答請見 234 頁

處理溝通障礙
Dealing with Communication Difficulties

At the office, and in the business world in general, it's vital to make sure there is no miscommunication on important matters. It's essential to ensure that you've properly understood the other person's meaning and vital to know that he or she has understood what you've said. With so much at stake, and the possibilities for miscommunication endless, it's fortunate for you that there are several excellent phrases in English for ensuring clarity.

在辦公室與一般商場中，確認在重要事項上沒有溝通不良至為重要。確定切實了解對方的意思並知道他或她了解你說的話是絕對必要的。既然事關緊要，溝通不良的可能性又無窮無盡，還好有一些很好用的英文詞語可用來確認事情清楚明瞭。

Biz 必通句型 Need-to-Know Phrases

1.1 表達困惑 Expressing Confusion

 track 29

❶I don't understand.
我不明白。
例 I'm sorry, I don't understand.
抱歉，我不明白。

❷I didn't get/<u>catch</u> that.
我沒聽清楚。
例 I didn't catch that. Could you say it again?
我沒聽清楚。你可不可以再說一遍？

❸I didn't hear what you said.
我沒聽到你說什麼。
例 Sorry, Todd. I didn't hear what you said.
對不起，陶德，我沒聽到你說什麼。

❹I'm not sure what you mean.
我不確定你是什麼意思。
例 I'm not sure what you mean, Sam.
我不確定你是什麼意思，山姆。

 ord List

catch [kætʃ] v. 聽懂；了解

❺ I don't <u>follow</u> you.

我不懂你的意思。

例 Excuse me. I don't follow you.

對不起，我不懂你的意思。

❻ What did you mean by (sth.)?

你說（某東西）是什麼意思？

例 What did you mean by "<u>realistic</u>?"

你說「實際」是什麼意思？

❼ I'm confused.

我搞不懂。

例 Wait a minute — I'm confused.

等一下，我搞不懂。

❽ I'm lost.

我一頭霧水。

例 I'm lost. Please say that again.

我一頭霧水，請再說一遍。

ord List

follow [ˋfɑlo] *v.* 聽得懂（說明等）

realistic [ˌriəˋlɪstɪk] *adj.* 現實的；實際的

1.2 詢問聽者是否了解 Asking if the Listener Understands

❶ Do you understand?

你懂嗎？

例 Do you understand what I am saying?

你懂不懂我在說什麼？

❷ Is that clear?

這樣清楚嗎？

例 Is that clear, Nancy?

這樣清楚嗎，南西？

❸ Do you know what I mean?

你知道我是什麼意思嗎？

例 Do you know what I mean when I say "deliberate?"

你知道我說的「刻意」是什麼意思嗎？

❹ Are you following me?

你懂我的意思嗎？

例 Are you following me so far?

你懂我的意思嗎？

 ord List

deliberate [dɪˋlɪbərɪt] *adj.* 刻意的；有計畫的

❺ Are you with me?

你聽得懂我在說什麼嗎？

例 Dennis, are you with me?

　　丹尼斯，你聽得懂我在說什麼嗎？

❻ Got that?

懂嗎？

例 Got that, everybody?

　　懂嗎，各位？

❼ Am I going too fast?

我會不會說得太快？

例 Ben you look confused. Am I going too fast?

　　班，你一臉茫然。我會不會說得太快？

❽ Any questions?

有問題嗎？

例 That's the end of my presentation. Any questions?

　　我的簡報到此為止。有問題嗎？

2 實戰會話 Show Time

2.1 專案設計圖出問題（1）
Problems with the Project Designs I

track 30

After working overtime and weekends for a solid month, the team developing the designs for the German project makes their deadline. However, shortly after the team begins <u>congratulating itself on</u> a job welldone, Darren receives a call from Germany.

Darren: Hello, Darren speaking.

Schneider: This is Heinz Schneider from Germany. I'm afraid I have some bad news for you.

Darren: Sorry, Mr. Schneider, I didn't catch that. It's pretty noisy in the office right now. Everyone is quite happy about our project. What was that, again?

Schneider: I said I have some bad news. There are some problems with your application for approval.

Darren: I don't understand. What do you mean by "problems?"

Schneider: Well, one problem is that you haven't <u>supplied</u> us <u>with</u> all the proper documents. In our regulations, under <u>subsection</u> X543.2, your company has to...

Darren: I'm sorry. Could you repeat that subsection number again for me?

Schneider: Yes, the number is X543.2.

Darren: OK, I got it. I'm with you so far.

Schneider: According to our regulations, you must provide us with three copies of each <u>relevant</u> document, an environmental study, plus two independent <u>estimates</u> of the <u>impact</u> of the project.

> Darren: Excuse me, Mr. Schneider, could you please speak a little more slowly. I need to write this information down.
>
> Schneider: Certainly, no problem.

譯文

在整整一個月超時工作和週末加班後，繪製德國專案設計圖的團隊趕上了最後期限。然而整個團隊才剛開始慶幸自己做得不錯，達倫就接到來自德國那邊的一通電話。

達倫：　　喂，我是達倫。

史奈德：我是德國的漢斯·史奈德。我恐怕有些壞消息要告訴你。

達倫：　　抱歉，史奈德先生，我沒聽清楚。現在辦公室裡滿吵的，大家都很滿意我們的專案。你剛說什麼請再說一次？

史奈德：我說我有些壞消息。你們的核准申請有些問題。

達倫：　　我不明白。你說「有問題」是什麼意思？

史奈德：嗯，問題之一就是你們還沒提供我們所有該繳交的文件。在我們的法規中，根據 X543.2 條款，貴公司必須……

達倫：　　對不起，你能重複一次那個條款號碼嗎？

史奈德：可以，號碼是 X543.2。

達倫：　　好，我知道了。到目前為止我都聽懂了。

史奈德：根據我們的法規，你們必須提供各相關文件一式三份、一項環境研究，外加兩個專案影響的獨立評估報告。

達倫：　　抱歉，史奈德先生，可不可以請你說慢一些，我需要把這些資訊寫下來。

史奈德：當然，沒問題。

Ｗord List

congratulate oneself on sth. 慶幸自己……

supply sb. with sth. 提供（某物）給（某人）

subsection [ˈsʌb.sɛkʃən] *n.* 細目；分款

relevant [ˈrɛləvənt] *adj.* 有關聯的；切題的

estimate [ˈɛstəmet] *n.* 估算；估價

impact [ˈɪmpækt] *n.* 影響（力）

2.2 專案設計圖出問題（2）
Problems with the Project Designs II

Amidst a team in celebration, Darren *struggles* to pay attention to the voice on the line.

Schneider: So, Darren, are you with me? Am I going too fast?

Darren: Actually, I'm lost. I didn't hear what you said about the designs not being detailed enough?

Schneider: Most of the design work is fine, but we must have more information related to pollution. Specifically, we need more details about the emissions. Any questions?

Darren: I see. I can send you some more information later today on that.

Schneider: If you do that, then I should be able to submit your application again. If everything is in order, we should approve your project within three months.

Darren: Three months? I don't understand. I thought the process took less than a month.

Schneider: It only takes a few weeks for small projects. However, your project is quite large and could have a big impact on the environment. For this kind of an application, the review is more complicated and takes longer.

Darren: I understand. That's really unexpected. Thanks for your help on this Mr. Schneider and I hope you can speed up the application process for us.

Schneider: I will try. Goodbye, Darren.

在團隊的一片慶祝氣氛中，達倫努力地把注意力集中在電話線上的聲音。

史奈德：那，達倫，你聽懂我在說什麼吧？我會不會說得太快？

達倫：　事實上我一頭霧水。我沒聽到你說什麼關於設計圖不夠精細的？

史奈德：設計方面大部分都沒問題，但是關於污染的部分我們需要更多資訊。說得更明確一點，我們需要更多關於排放物的細節。有問題嗎？

達倫：　我懂了。我今天稍晚可以把更多相關資訊寄給你。

史奈德：如果你能這麼做，我應該可以再幫你們提出一次申請。如果一切順利，我們應該會在三個月內批准你們的專案。

達倫：　三個月？我不明白，我以為整個過程要不到一個月。

史奈德：小型專案是只要幾週，但是你們的專案挺大的，可能會對環境造成重大影響。對於這類的申請，審核會更複雜、費時更久。

達倫：　我明白了。這真是始料未及。謝謝你幫忙這件事，史奈德先生，希望你能夠幫我們加速申請過程。

史奈德：我會試試看。再見，達倫。

 ord List

amidst [ə`mɪdst] *prep.*【文語】在⋯⋯之中
struggle [`strʌgl] *v.* 掙扎著（要⋯⋯）
detailed [`di`teld] *adj.* 詳細的
emission [ɪ`mɪʃən] *n.* 排出物（質）
submit [səb`mɪt] *v.* （向⋯⋯）提出
approve [ə`pruv] *v.* （正式的）核准；批准
speed up 加速⋯⋯

3　Biz 加分句型 Nice-to-Know Phrases

3.1　表示你了解 Showing You Understand

 track 31

❶ I understand.
我明白了。
例 Yes, I understand what you are saying.
是的，我明白你在說什麼了。

❷ I see.
我懂了。
例 I see. That's interesting.
我懂了，很有趣。

❸ I got it.
我知道了。
例 OK, I got it.
好，我知道了。

❹ I'm with you.
我聽得懂你在說什麼。
例 I'm with you — keep going.
我聽得懂你在說什麼，繼續說。

3.2 要求說話者重複某事或說慢點
Asking the Speaker to Repeat Something or Slow Down

❶ What was that again?

你剛說什麼請再說一次？

例 Excuse me, what was that again?

對不起，你剛說什麼請再說一次？

❷ Could you repeat that, please?

能不能麻煩你重複一次？

例 Could you repeat that, please? I'm not sure what you mean.

能不能麻煩你重複一次？我不確定你是什麼意思。

❸ Please speak a little more slowly.

請稍微說慢一些。

例 I'm sorry, please speak a little more slowly.

對不起，請稍微說慢一些。

❹ You're speaking too fast for me.

你說話的速度對我而言太快了。

例 My English isn't so good. You're speaking too fast for me.

我的英文沒那麼好，你說話的速度對我而言太快了。

:::::::: 小心陷阱 ::::::::

☹ 錯誤用法：

What is your meaning "problems?"

你說「有問題」是什麼意思？

☺ 正確用法：

What do you mean by "problems?"

你說「有問題」是什麼意思？

:::::::: Biz 一點通 ::::::::

Not understanding something can be embarrassing for some people, and these individuals often feel shy about expressing confusion. Keep in mind though that not admitting your lack of understanding puts you at the risk of missing important points. Ask yourself: Is it more embarrassing to ask a question or to <u>blow</u> a major case? If you don't understand something, it's better to tell the person earlier than waste time later. As the phrase goes, "There are no stupid questions."

對某些人來說，聽不懂某件事可能滿丟臉的，而這些人常常不好意思表示自己的困惑。但是記住，不承認自己不了解會讓你承受錯失重點的風險。請自問：是提出問題還是搞砸一件大案子比較丟臉？如果你不明白某件事，早點告訴對方好過之後浪費時間。正如俗話所說的：「世上沒有笨問題。」

ord List

....

blow [blo] *v.* 搞砸

4 實戰演練 Practice Exercises

Ⅰ 請為下列詞語選出最適合本章的中文譯義。

❶ at stake

(A) 搬家中　(B) 熱賣中　(C) 成為問題

❷ I didn't catch that.

(A) 我沒有聽清楚。　(B) 我沒趕上。　(C) 我沒有逮到它。

❸ have an impact on

(A) 對⋯⋯加以控制　(B) 對⋯⋯有影響　(C) 干擾⋯⋯

Ⅱ 你會如何回應下面兩句話？

❶ I don't follow you.

(A) I'm lost.

(B) Where are you going?

(C) Let me repeat that.

❷ I didn't get that.

(A) Let me say that again.

(B) Me too.

(C) Here you go.

Ⅲ 請用下列詞語寫出一篇簡短的對話。

I don't follow you.	I'm lost
Do you know what I mean?	I see
Could you repeat that, please?	What did you mean by?

＊解答請見 235 頁

第 **11** 章

處理批評
Handling Criticism

One of the hardest things to deal with in life is criticism. When you give or receive criticism, a lot of emotion and embarrassment can cloud and confuse the issue, resulting in misunderstanding or hurt feelings. Therefore, you need to be objective if you criticize some-one or need to point out a problem or mistake. If you are to blame for a problem, then it's professional to accept criticism and offer assurances that mistakes won't happen again. When used construc-tively, criticism is a tool that can help improve the quality and con-sistency of a team's work.

人生中最難面對的事物之一就是批評。當你批評別人或接受別人批評時，大量的情緒與尷尬可能會矇蔽、混淆主題，而導致誤解或傷害感情。因此，在你批評別人或必須指出某一問題或錯誤時，必須客觀。如果你該為某個錯誤負責，那麼專業的做法就是接受批評，並保證錯誤不會再發生。當批評能以一種具建設性的方式來處理時，它可以是一個幫助改善團隊工作品質和一致性的工具。

Biz 必通句型 Need-to-Know Phrases

track 32

1.1 批評 Criticizing

找出誰應該負責

❶ How did this happen?

這是怎麼發生的？

例 How did this happen? What went wrong?

這是怎麼發生的？哪裡出了錯？

❷ Who did this?

這是誰做的？

例 Who did this? Fanny, do you know?

這是誰做的？芬妮，妳知道嗎？

❸ Who's to blame?

應該怪誰？

例 Who's to blame for breaking the printer?

印表機弄壞了該怪誰？

❹ Who's at fault?

誰有錯？

例 Who forgot to bring the projector? Who's at fault here?

誰忘記帶投影機來？這件事誰有錯？

ord List

be to blame 應受譴責；應負責任

at fault 有過失的；有過錯的

142

指責犯錯者

❺ It's your fault.

是你的錯。

例 Tony, it's your fault. You should have been more careful.

東尼,是你的錯,你應該要更小心的。

❻ It was your responsibility.

是你的責任。

例 Brenda, it was your responsibility to keep the staff room clean.

布蘭達,保持員工休息室整潔是妳的責任。

❼ You should have (done sth.)

你應該（做某件事）。

例 You should have bought more paper for the fax machine.

你應該買更多傳真紙的。

❽ Why didn't you...?

你為什麼沒有……?

例 Why didn't you finish that assignment on time?

你為什麼沒有準時完成那項任務?

1.2 接受與否認批評 Accepting and Rejecting Criticism

接受批評

❶ I'm to blame.

應該怪我。

例 I'm to blame for breaking the computer.

電腦弄壞了該怪我。

❷ It's my fault.

是我的錯。

例 I lost the report. It's my fault.

我弄丟了報告，是我的錯。

❸ I did it.

是我做的。

例 I'm sorry. I did it.

對不起，是我做的。

❹ I'm responsible.

我該負責。

例 I'm responsible for <u>missing the deadline</u>.

我該為沒趕上最後期限負責。

W ord List

miss the deadline 沒趕上最後期限

否認批評

⑤It wasn't me.

不是我。

例 It wasn't me who left the <u>briefcase</u> on the train.

把公事包忘在火車上的不是我。

⑥Don't blame me.

別怪我。

例 Did I drop the camera? No. Don't blame me.

我有沒有把相機掉在地上？沒有，別怪我。

⑦It must have been someone else.

一定是別人。

例 It must have been someone else who did it.

一定是別人做的。

⑧I <u>had nothing to do with</u> (sth.)（強烈否認）

（某件事）與我無關。

例 I had nothing to do with making the client angry.

把客戶惹火的事與我無關。

ord List

briefcase [ˋbrif͵kes] *n.* 公事包

have nothing to do with... 與⋯⋯無關

2 實戰會話 Show Time

2.1 錯過期限 The Missed Deadline

Because of the problems with the design application to Germany, Darren's team has missed its first important deadline, which <u>threatens</u> to delay the whole project. WHT's head engineer, Simon has called a meeting to discuss the problem.

Simon: Good morning, everyone. I'm quite disappointed that we've missed the deadline that was set for the approval of the designs. How did this happen?

Steve: As team leader, I'm responsible. However, I think that there was just too much work to do in a very short time.

Simon: Wait a minute, Steve. I don't really think it's your fault. I think it's very important to find out who is to blame for this, so it doesn't happen again. I understand that there was a problem with the documents given to the German government. Steve, who did this?

Steve: Well, it was a team effort, but I had asked Darren specifically to make sure the documents were in order.

Simon: That's what I had heard. Darren, why didn't you ensure all the necessary documents were sent?

Darren: I was a little unclear on some of the regulations — they are very complicated.

Simon: You should have asked someone about them. It was your responsibility to check the regulations.

Darren: I guess you're right. It's my fault.

由於向德國申請設計圖的核准出了問題，達倫的團隊沒趕上第一個重要的期
限，因此很可能會被迫把整個專案往後延。 WHT 的總工程師賽門召開了一場會
議討論這個問題。

賽門：　各位早。我很失望我們沒趕上設計圖核准的期限。這是怎麼發生的？

史提夫：身為團隊領導人，我該負責。但是，我認為在這麼短的時間內要做的
　　　　事情太多了。

賽門：　等一下，史提夫，我並不認為是你的錯。我認為找出誰該為此負責很
　　　　重要，這種事才不會再發生。我知道給德國政府的文件出了問題。史
　　　　提夫，這是誰做的？

史提夫：嗯，那是團隊共同的努力，但是我有特別請達倫要確保文件都準備好
　　　　了。

賽門：　我也是這麼聽說的。達倫，你為什麼沒有確認所有必要的文件都送出
　　　　去了呢？

達倫：　我對某些法規不太清楚，它們非常複雜。

賽門：　你應該問問別人的，確認法規是你的責任。

達倫：　我想你說得對，是我的錯。

Ｗ ord List

threaten [ˈθrɛtn̩] *v.* 威脅；脅迫

2.2 怪罪遊戲 The Blame Game

As the meeting continues, more questions are <u>raised</u> about why the deadline was missed.

Steve: Actually, Simon, I don't think Darren is entirely at fault for missing the deadline. Other people made mistakes as well. For example, Brenda was a little late with some of the translations.

Brenda: That's not fair, Steve. I had nothing to do with missing the deadline. Some translations were late because I wasn't given them until very late. I remember that Laura delayed sending me some translations for a few days. Don't blame me.

Laura: It wasn't me. I was always on time. It must have been someone else. I think Steve was right when he said it was his fault. Steve said Darren should help out with the designs, even though Darren doesn't have much experience.

Simon: It wasn't Steve. I think Steve is trying to <u>protect</u> Darren. Darren, there's no <u>excuse</u> for it. Don't let it happen again.

Darren: I'm sorry to disappoint everyone. It won't happen again. I've learned from my mistake.

Simon: Good, Darren. I'm very glad to hear that. Now, let's work harder and <u>get this project back on schedule</u>.

隨著會議的持續進行，更多關於為何期限沒能趕上的疑問浮上檯面。

史提夫：事實上，賽門，我不覺得期限沒趕上完全是達倫的過失。其他人也有犯錯，譬如布蘭達部分的翻譯就有點延遲。

布蘭達：這樣說不公平，史提夫，最後期限沒趕上與我無關。有些翻譯之所以會延遲，是因為我到很後來才拿到它們。我記得蘿拉晚了幾天才把一些翻譯給我。別怪我。

蘿拉：　不是我，我一向準時交差，一定是別人。我認為史提夫說是他的錯是對的。雖然達倫沒什麼經驗，史提夫還是說他應該幫忙作設計圖。

賽門：　不是史提夫。我想史提夫是想保護達倫。達倫，這件事你沒有藉口。別讓它再發生。

達倫：　抱歉讓大家失望，不會再發生了。我已經從自己的錯誤中學到了教訓。

賽門：　很好，達倫，我很高興聽你這麼說。現在，大家再努力一點，把這項專案的進度趕上。

ord List

....

raise [rez] *v.* 提出（質詢；異議等）

protect [prə`tɛkt] *v.* 保護

excuse [ɪk`skjuz] *n.* 藉口；理由

get sth. back on schedule 使某事務趕上原進度

track 34

3 Biz 加分句型 Nice-to-Know Phrases

3.1 使用強烈批評 Using Strong Criticism

❶ That's <u>unacceptable</u>.
那是無法接受的。
例 That's unacceptable to me.
那對我來說是無法接受的。

❷ There's no excuse for (sth.)
（某件事）沒有藉口。
例 There's no excuse for what you did.
你做的事情沒有藉口。

❸ It's <u>inexcusable</u>.
這是不可原諒的。
例 It's inexcusable that you have been late so many times.
你遲到了這麼多次是不可原諒的。

❹ Don't let it happen again.（警告）
別讓它再發生。
例 You forgot to attend the meeting. Don't let it happen again.
你忘了參與會議。別讓它再發生。

ord List
···
unacceptable [ˌʌnək`sɛptəbl] *adj.* 不能接受的；無法接納的
inexcusable [ˌɪnɪk`skjuzəbl] *adj.* 無法辯解的；不能原諒的

3.2 提供保證 Offering <u>Assurances</u>

❶ It won't happen again.
不會再發生了。
例 I promise it won't happen again.
　　我保證不會再發生了。

❷ I won't repeat the same mistake.
我不會再犯同樣的錯。
例 I <u>guarantee</u> I won't repeat the same mistake.
　　我保證不會再犯同樣的錯。

❸ This is the last time....
這是最後一次……。
例 This is the last time I will forget to bring the report.
　　這是我最後一次忘記帶報告。

❹ I've learned from my mistake.
我已經從自己的錯誤中學到了教訓。
例 Don't worry, I've learned from my mistake.
　　別擔心，我已經從自己的錯誤中學到了教訓。

ord List

assurances [əˋʃurəns] *n.* 保證；擔保
guarantee [͵gærənˋti] *v.* 保證

:::::::::: 小心陷阱 ::::::::::

☹ 錯誤用法：

I am **blamed** for the mistake.

這個過錯應該怪我。

☺ 正確用法：

I am **to blame** for the mistake.

這個過錯應該怪我。

:::::::::: Biz 一點通 ::::::::::

When you criticize, it's useful to <u>target</u> the problem, and not the person. For example, it's better to say, "Your performance needs improving," rather than "You are <u>incompetent</u>." The former statement is more <u>constructive</u> and causes less emotional damage than the latter. Likewise, if someone is criticising you personally, try to direct the criticism towards actions and performance, and find out specifically what you are doing that the criticizer doesn't like.

當你在批評時，要對事不對人才有用。例如，最好說：「你的表現需要改進」，而不要說：「你真無能。」前面的說法比後面的更具有建設性，造成的情緒傷害也比較小。同樣地，如果一個人對你作人身攻擊，試著將批評導向行動與表現，並明確找出批評者不喜歡你做的究竟是什麼事情。

ord List

target [ˋtɑrgɪt] *v.* 以⋯⋯為目標；對⋯⋯瞄準

incompetent [ɪnˋkɑmpətənt] *adj.* 無能的；不能勝任的

constructive [kənˋstrʌktɪv] *adj.* 建設性的；積極的

4 實戰演練 Practice Exercises

I 請為下列詞語選出適合本章的中文譯義。

❶ at fault

(A) 追究過失 (B) 有過失的 (C) 不良的

❷ I'm to blame.

(A) 我要怪罪他人。 (B) 應該怪我。 (C) 我要開罵了。

❸ no excuse

(A) 沒有道歉 (B) 沒有憑藉 (C) 沒有藉口

II 你會如何回應下面這兩句話？

❶ Who did this?

(A) It was your responsibility.

(B) It's my fault.

(C) That's unacceptable.

❷ It's your fault.

(A) How did it happen?

(B) Who's to blame?

(C) It won't happen again.

III 請用下列詞語寫出一篇簡短的對話。

How did this happen?	It's your fault.
It was your responsibility.	That's unacceptable.
I'm to blame.	I won't repeat the same mistake.

＊解答請見 236 頁

道歉與解釋
Apologizing and Explaining

To maintain good relations at work, you need to know when to apologize if you've made a mistake, and when it's appropriate to explain your actions. Sometimes, you do things unintentionally and an error or problem occurs. Other times, mistakes or accidents are just unavoidable. In all of these instances, there are some phrases in English that help the listener better understand your explanations. These phrases act as a framework for your message.

要在工作職場上保持良好關係,你就需要知道如果犯了錯何時該道歉,何時又該適切解釋你的行為。有時你並非故意要做一些事情,而錯誤或問題就這麼發生了;其他時候,錯誤或意外是無法避免的。所有的這些狀況都有一些英文用語可幫助聽者更了解你所做的說明。這些詞語可作為你想傳達的訊息的架構。

1 Biz 必通句型 Need-to-Know Phrases

1.1 道歉 Apologizing

❶ Sorry about that.（用於不太重要的小事）
那件事很抱歉。
例 I forgot to bring that DVD for you — sorry about that. I'll bring it tomorrow.
我忘記幫你把那片 DVD 帶來，抱歉。我明天會帶來。

❷ I'm sorry (for sth.)
我很抱歉（某件事）。
例 I'm sorry for wasting your time.
我很抱歉浪費你的時間。

❸ I apologize (for sth.)
（因某件事），我道歉。
例 I apologize for being late.
我遲到了，我道歉。

❹ Please forgive me.
請原諒我。
例 Mary, I lost your book. Please forgive me.
瑪莉，我把妳的書弄丟了。請原諒我。

❺I regret (sth.)

我很遺憾（某件事）

　例 I regret breaking your fax machine.

　　我很遺憾弄壞了你的傳真機。

❻I let you down.（用於使某人失望時）

我讓你失望了。

　例 Belinda, I did a poor job on that report. I let you down.

　　白琳達，我那份報告作得很糟。我讓妳失望了。

❼I feel very bad (about sth.)（表示強烈遺憾）

（關於某件事）我覺得很過意不去。

　例 I feel very bad about damaging your car.

　　弄壞你的車我覺得很過意不去。

❽I'm terribly sorry (about sth.)（表示極為強烈的遺憾）

（關於某件事）我非常抱歉。

　例 I'm terribly sorry about forgetting our meeting.

　　忘了我們的會議我非常抱歉。

Ⓦord List

....

regret [rɪˋgrɛt] *v.* 懊悔；因……而遺憾 (~ +V-ing)

let sb. down 讓某人失望

damage [ˋdæmɪdʒ] *v./n.* 損害；損傷

1.2 解釋 Explaining

❶ The reason is....
原因是……。
例 Sorry, I'm late. The reason is I had a meeting.
抱歉，我遲到了。原因是我之前在開會。

❷ It's because (reason).
這是因為（原因）。
例 I feed very bad about not helping you. It's because I had too much work to do.
沒幫你我覺得很難過。因為我要做的工作太多了。

❸ As a result (sth. happened).
結果（某事發生）。
例 I slept in. As a result, I missed the train.
我睡過頭，結果錯過了火車。

❹ As a consequence.... / Consequently....
結果……。
例 You didn't work hard enough. Consequently, we lost the deal.
你工作得不夠努力，結果使得我們失去了這筆生意。

ord List

sleep in 睡過頭
consequence [ˋkɑnsəˏkwɛns] *n.* 後果；結局
consequently [ˋkɑnsəˏkwɛntlɪ] *adv.* 結果；因此

❺ (Sth./Sb.) was the cause (of sth.).
造成（某事）的原因是（某事／某人）。
例 The poor economy was the cause of the business failure.
造成生意失敗的原因是經濟不景氣。

❻ (Sth.); therefore (sth.).
（某事），因此（某事）。
例 He is not <u>qualified</u>; therefore he didn't get the job.
他資格不符，因此沒得到這份工作。

❼ (Sth.); thus (sth.).
（某事），所以（某事）。
例 He worked very hard; thus he got a promotion.
他工作得非常賣力，所以他獲得了升遷。

❽ (Sth.); <u>hence</u> (sth.).
（某事），因此（某事）。
例 The company did very well this year; hence we got a very good bonus.
公司今年業績很好，因此我們拿到很不錯的紅利。

ord List

qualified [ˋkwɑləˌfaɪd] *adj.* 有資格的；合格的
hence [hɛns] *adv.* 因此

2 實戰會話 Show Time

 track 36

2.1 道歉 Apologizing

After the meeting to discuss the missed deadline, Darren feels very bad. He decides to arrange a <u>separate</u>, <u>private</u> meeting with Simon to discuss things further.

Simon: Hello, Darren. Come on in. What can I do for you?

Darren: Hi Simon. I feel very bad about the problem we had with the designs. I let you down, and I'm sorry.

Simon: Yes, it was a big mistake, and I hope it doesn't affect the rest of the project too much. Do you know how you made the error?

Darren: I think the reason is that I haven't had a lot of experience with these kinds of approvals. As a consequence, I wasn't sure about all of the <u>procedures</u> to follow. I didn't mean to do it.

Simon: I know, Darren. People don't usually mean to make mistakes.

Darren: You're right. Even though it wasn't <u>intentional</u>, I still made a mistake. I'm disappointed in myself. My inexperience was the cause.

Simon: Well, don't worry about it too much. Just try to improve your performance in the future. I appreciate you coming to my office to talk about it.

在開會討論錯過期限的事之後，達倫覺得很過意不去。他決定和賽門另外安排一個私下的會議，作進一步的討論。

賽門： 哈囉，達倫，進來吧。有何貴幹？

達倫： 嗨，賽門。我們的設計圖出問題我覺得很過意不去。我讓你失望了，很抱歉。

賽門： 是的，那的確是個大錯誤。我希望它不會給專案的其他部分帶來太大的影響。你知道自己是怎麼犯下這個錯的嗎？

達倫： 我想原因是我對這類核准案還沒有太多的經驗，以致於不太了解所有要依循的程序。我不是有意的。

賽門： 我知道，達倫，人通常都不是故意要犯錯的。

達倫： 你說得對。縱然我不是故意的，但是還是犯了錯。我對自己很失望。我缺乏經驗是原因。

賽門： 嗯，不要想太多，只要以後試著改善你的表現就好了。謝謝你到我辦公室來談這件事。

separate [ˈsɛpərɪt] *adj.* 個別的；單獨的
private [ˈpraɪvɪt] *adj.* 私下的；非公開的
procedure [prəˈsidʒə] *n.* 手續；程序
intentional [ɪnˈtɛʃənl] *adj.* 故意的；有企圖的

2.2 解釋 Explaining

In order to cheer Darren up, Steve has organized a dinner with all the team members on the German project. Darren still feels he has to apologize, but the others want him to feel happy.

Steve: Thanks for coming everybody. How are you doing, Darren?

Darren: <u>So-so</u>. I still regret making those mistakes. I didn't sleep very well. Consequently, I feel a little tired.

Laura: Don't worry so much, Darren. It's just one mistake.

Brenda runs up to the table, awkwardly holding a stack of file folders.

Brenda: Hi, I apologize for being late.

Brenda bumps the table, drops the files, and <u>spills</u> a glass of water.

Brenda: Oops. Sorry about that.

Steve: Why were you late, Brenda?

Brenda: Oh, it's because I had to work overtime. I have to prepare for a meeting tomorrow morning; therefore I had to spend some extra time at the office talking to Paul about the meeting. What was everyone talking about before I came?

Darren: I was just saying I'm terribly sorry for making our team miss the deadline. It's not like me at all. I don't know what happened.

Brenda: It's not that bad. Cheer up. It was an accident. You didn't <u>do it on purpose</u>.

Darren: Thanks for being <u>understanding</u>.

譯 文

為了讓達倫開心起來，史提夫辦了一個晚餐聚會，所有德國專案的團隊成員都出席了。達倫還是覺得自己得道歉，但是其他人希望他開心起來。

史提夫：謝謝大家來。你還好嗎，達倫？

達倫：　還好。我還是很懊惱犯了那些錯。我沒睡好，結果覺得有點累。

蘿拉：　別太擔心，達倫，那只是一個錯誤而已。

布蘭達跑向桌子這邊，笨手笨腳地抱著一疊檔案夾。

布蘭達：嗨，我遲到了，我道歉。

布蘭達撞到桌子，弄掉了檔案夾，還打翻了一杯水。

布蘭達：糟糕，抱歉。

史提夫：妳為什麼遲到，布蘭達？

布蘭達：喔，因為我得加班。因為我得準備明天早上要開的一個會，所以必須在辦公室多待一會兒和保羅討論會議的事。在我來之前大家在聊些什麼？

達倫：　我正在說我非常抱歉讓我們的團隊錯過最後期限。那一點都不像我。我不知道怎麼了。

布蘭達：沒有那麼糟。振作起來。那是個意外，你不是故意那麼做的。

達倫：　謝謝大家這麼體諒。

ord List

so-so [`so, so] *adj./adv.*【口語】普普通通；還過得去

spill [spɪl] *v.* 使……溢出、散落

do sth. on purpose　故意做某事

understanding [ˌʌndəˋstændɪŋ] *adj.* 能諒解的；寬容的

3 Biz 加分句型 Nice-to-Know Phrases

 track 37

3.1 找藉口 Giving Excuses

❶ It was an accident.
那是個意外。
例 Excuse me. It was an accident.
　　對不起,那是個意外。

❷ I didn't mean to (do sth.).
我不是故意(做某件事)。
例 I didn't mean to hit you. Sorry.
　　我不是故意要打你,抱歉。

❸ I didn't do it on purpose.
我不是故意那麼做的。
例 I didn't do it on purpose, Jean. <u>Give me a break</u>.
　　我不是故意那麼做的,琴。饒了我吧。

❹ It wasn't intentional.
那不是故意的。
例 It wasn't intentional — it was an accident.
　　那不是故意的,那是個意外。

 ord List
Give me a break. 饒了我吧。

3.2 表現悔意 Showing Regret

❶I made a mistake.

我犯了一個錯誤。

例 I made a mistake — please forgive me.

我犯了一個錯誤，請原諒我。

❷I'm disappolnted in myself.

我對自己很失望。

例 I'm disappointed in myself for losing the camera.

弄掉了相機，我對自己很失望。

❸It wasn't like me at all.（表示自己的行為是不尋常的表現）

那一點都不像我。

例 I don't know why I got mad. It wasn't like me at all to do that.

我不知道自己為何發飆。那一點都不像我。

❹I don't know what happened.（表示不敢相信自己的行為）

我不知道我是怎麼了。

例 I'm terribly sorry — I don't know whal happened.

非常抱歉，我不知道我是怎麼了。

:::::::: 小心陷阱 ::::::::

☹ 錯誤用法：

I'm disappointed **for** myself.

我對自己很失望。

☺ 正確用法：

I'm disappointed **in** myself.

我對自己很失望。

:::::::: Biz 一點通 ::::::::

While it's important to <u>acknowledge</u> a mistake that you have made on the job and apologize for it, it's best not to <u>dwell</u> on it and overly apologize — in the Show Time dialogs, Darren was starting to apologize too much, and his team members stopped him. It's good to admit the mistake, promise not to repeat it (as seen in Chapter 11, "Offering Assurances"), and then work on doing a good job rather than continually regretting the mistake that you made.

雖然承認自己在工作上犯了錯並為此道歉很重要，但是最好不要放不下而過度道歉。在實戰對話裡，達倫就開始有道歉太多的跡象，而他的團隊阻止了他。承認犯錯，保證不會再犯（就像第十一章「提供保證」那樣），然後努力把工作做好，不繼續懊悔自己犯的錯才是正確的。

Ⓦord List

acknowledge [əkˋnɑlɪdʒ] v. 承認……為事實；招認

dwell on... 細想……；仔細研究……

4 實戰演練 Practice Exercises

Ⅰ 請為下列詞語選出最適合本章的中文譯義。

❶ as a result

(A) 結果　(B) 結束　(C) 歸因於

❷ I didn't do it on purpose.

(A) 我漫無目的。　(B) 我並非故意的。　(C) 我未被要求這樣做。

❸ dwell on a mistake

(A) 推託過失　(B) 老想著過失　(C) 被錯誤拖累

Ⅱ 你會如何回應下面這兩句話？

❶ It was an accident.

(A) That's OK.

(B) Where is the accident?

(C) I'm terribly sorry.

❷ I feel very bad about breaking your camera.

(A) You should take some medicine.

(B) Have you seen a doctor?

(C) Don't worry about it.

Ⅲ 請用下列詞語寫出一段簡短的對話。

I apologize	please forgive me.
the reason is	it's because
I didn't mean to	therefore

＊解答請見 237 頁

談論職場事務
Talking About Workplace Events

When it comes to workplace events, there are a lot of specific phrases and vocabulary items that are used to convey information. In this chapter we will survey some very common words and terms used in everyday office conversation. Knowing them and incorporating them into your lexicon will help you keep up to date with what's going on in the office.

談論職場事務時，有許多特定的片語和字彙可用來傳達資訊。在本章中，我們將檢視日常辦公室對話裡非常常用的一些字詞。如果你認識它們並把它們納入你的字彙裡，將能幫助你隨時掌握辦公室裡發生的事。

1 Biz 必通句型 Need-to-Know Phrases

1.1 談論工作相關事務
Talking About Job Events

---

❶ The salary is (adj.)
薪水（形容詞）。
例 The salary is pretty good.
　薪水還不錯。

---

❷ How is the pay...?
……給的薪水如何？
例 How is the pay at Yoyodyne?
　優達因給的薪水如何？

---

❸ ...have to work (a lot of) overtime.
…… 必須（大量）加班。
例 I had to work a lot of overtime last week.
　我上禮拜必須大量加班。

---

❹ ...got a promotion.
……升官了。
例 Stanley got a promotion yesterday.
　史丹利昨天升官了。

---

❺**What are the <u>benefits</u> (of this job)?**
（工作的）福利有什麼？
例 What are the benefits of this job?
　這份工作的福利有什麼？

❻**This company has a (adj.) <u>medical</u>/<u>dental</u> plan.**
這家公司有（形容詞）醫療險／牙科險。
例 This company has a great medical plan.
　這家公司有很不錯的醫療險。

❼**...think of changing jobs.**
……考慮換工作。
例 I'm thinking of changing jobs.
　我在考慮換工作。

❽**...is going to <u>retire</u> (time).**
……（時間）要退休。
例 I heard Frank is going to retire this year.
　我聽說法蘭克今年要退休。

Word List

benefit [ˋbɛnəfɪt] *n.* 利益；好處
medical [ˋmɛdɪkl] *adj.* 醫療的
dental [ˋdɛntl] *adj.* 牙齒的；牙科的
retire [rɪˋtaɪr] *v.* 退休；退職

1.2 談論一般商業狀況 Talking About General Business

❶ The <u>competition</u> in (region) market is (adj.).
（區域）市場的競爭（形容詞）。

例 The competition in China market is pretty <u>tough</u>.
中國市場的競爭相當激烈。

❷ The market for (product) is (adj.).
（產品）市場（形容詞）。

例 The market for notebook computers is very good right now.
筆記型電腦的市場現在非常好。

❸ There is a demand for....
……有其需求。

例 There's a demand for portable printers.
手提印表機有其需求。

❹ We <u>made (a lot of) profit on</u>....
我們在 ……賺入（大筆）利潤。

例 We made a lot of profit on that item last month.
我們上個月在那個產品上賺入大筆利潤。

Word List

competition [ˌkɑmpəˋtɪʃən] *n.* 競爭

tough [tʌf] *adj.* 棘手的；費勁的

make a profit on... 在……上獲利

❺ ...is <u>forcasted</u> to improve (time).
……預測（時間）會好轉。
例 Sales are forecasted to improve next year.
業績預測明年會好轉。

❻ The <u>budget</u> for (sth.) is (adj.).
（某東西）的預算……。
例 The budget for this project is huge.
這項專案的預算非常龐大。

❼ ...is <u>booming</u>.
……正蓬勃發展。
例 Business is booming these days.
生意近日來正蓬勃發展。

❽ There has been a <u>decline</u> in....
……衰退了。
例 There's been a decline in sales recently.
最近銷售業績衰退了。

Word List
forcast [for`kæst] v. 預報（天氣）；預測 （未來等）
budget [`bʌdʒɪt] n. 預算
boom [bum] v. 突然繁榮起來；迅速增長
decline [dɪ`klaɪn] n. 下跌；衰退

2 實戰會話 Show Time

2.1 談論工作相關事務
Talking About Job Events

It's time again for the <u>ritual</u> afternoon coffee break and we find Darren and Sandra <u>cradling</u> <u>steaming</u> cups of coffee as they converse in the staff room.

Sandra: I've really had to work overtime this week. I'm starting to wonder if the salary is worth all the hard work we have to do.

Darren: Yes, I've worked hard, too. But I think the pay is pretty good, and the benefits, like the medical and dental plans, are not bad.

Sandra: I'm not as happy about this company as you are. Actually, I've been thinking of changing jobs.

Darren: Really? I think there are many chances to get a promotion at WHT. You should think about that as well.

Sandra: Maybe, but WHT is not a huge company. I think it will take a long time to get promoted. Right now there's a big demand for engineers with our kinds of skills. A few of the big engineering companies are <u>advertising for people</u>. I'm sure it wouldn't be too difficult to get hired.

Darren: But with big companies, you have to worry about getting <u>laid off</u>. Many only care about making big profits. Also, you have to worry about the <u>labor force</u> at those places <u>going on strike</u>.

Sandra: Well, it doesn't hurt to check out the opportunities.

又到了例行的下午休息喝咖啡的時間，我們看到達倫和珊德拉捧著冒著熱氣的咖啡，在員工休息室裡聊天。

珊德拉：我這個星期必須加不少班。我開始在想，不知道薪水到底值不值我們必須做那麼多苦工。

達倫：　是啊，我最近也工作得很辛苦。但是我覺得薪水還不錯，而且福利，像是醫療險和牙科險，也不差。

珊德拉：我對這家公司沒有像你那麼滿意。事實上，我一直在考慮要不要換工作。

達倫：　真的嗎？我覺得在 WHT 獲得升遷的機會很多，妳應該把這點也考慮進去。

珊德拉：也許吧，但是 WHT 不是一家大公司，我覺得要很久的時間才能得到升遷。現在具備我們這樣技能的工程師大有其需求，有幾家大型工程公司就在登廣告找人。我確定要被雇用不會是件難事。

達倫：　但是在大公司裡妳得擔心被裁員；許多大公司都只在乎賺入大筆利潤。而且妳還得擔心那些地方的勞工罷工。

珊德拉：嗯，看看這些機會還是無妨。

Word List

ritual [ˈrɪtʃʊəl] *adj.* 例行的；儀式的
cradle [ˈkredl] *v.*（用雙手等）捧
steaming [ˈstimɪŋ] *adj.* 冒著熱氣的
advertise for sb. 登廣告徵人
lay off 暫時解雇（人員）；裁員
labor force [ˈlebɚˈfors] *n.* 勞動力
go on strike 罷工

2.2 談論別家公司 Talking About Another Company

As Sandra and Darren <u>sip</u> coffee and talk, Paul enters with a giant latte and a <u>complacent</u> smile.

Darren: Hi. How are things going?

Paul: Great. Business is booming. The market for our engineering projects is really good right now, although there is also a lot of competition from other firms.

Sandra: Good to hear that. Say, Paul, I want to ask you if you know anything about a company called Sky-High Engineering.

Paul: I know that it is a big engineering firm that's in trouble. I've heard that it is really <u>in the red</u>. It wouldn't surprise me if that company went <u>bankrupt</u>. Why?

Sandra: Oh, I just saw an <u>ad</u> that they were looking to hire someone.

Paul: Experts forecast that the next quarter will be even worse for them. They can't keep control of their budget or expenses. I think they might <u>go out of business</u> soon. I wouldn't go to that company.

Sandra: I wouldn't either. Thanks for the information.

譯 文

在珊德拉和達倫一邊啜飲著咖啡、一邊聊天的時候，保羅拿著一杯大拿鐵走進來，臉上帶著一抹志得意滿的笑容。

達倫：　嗨。怎麼樣，事情都順利吧？

保羅：　好極了。生意蓬勃發展。雖然有很多其他公司和我們競爭，但是我們工程專案的市場現在相當好。

珊德拉：聽你這麼說真好。對了，保羅，我想問你，有一家叫天高工程的公司不知道你熟不熟。

保羅：　我知道的是，那是一家陷入麻煩的大型工程公司。我聽說那家公司現在負債累累，如果它破產，我也不會訝異。為什麼問？

珊德拉：喔，我只是看到一則廣告說他們要徵人。

保羅：　專家預測他們下一季會更糟。他們一直無法掌控他們的預算跟費用，我想他們可能很快就會倒閉。我是不會想去那公司的。

珊德拉：我也不會。謝謝你的資訊。

ord List

sip [sɪp] *v.* 啜；啜飲
complacent [kəm`plesn̩t] *adj.* 自滿的；自得的
in the red　有赤字；欠債
bankrupt [`bæŋkrʌpt] *adj.* 破產的
ad [æd] *n.*【口語】廣告 (= advertisement)
go out of business 停業；倒閉

177

3 Biz 加分句型 Nice-to-Know Phrases

 track 40

3.1 談論員工流動
Talking About Staff Changes

❶ ...get hired.
……被錄用。
例 Three people got hired last month at our company.
上個月我們公司錄用了三個人。

❷ ...take a leave of <u>absence</u>.
……請假。
例 Thomas is taking a leave of absence this month.
湯瑪斯這個月請假。

❸ ...get fired for....
……因為……被開除。
例 Sally got fired for being late all the time.
莎莉因為總是遲到而被開除。

❹ ...get laid off.
……被裁員。
例 Fifty people got laid off from GiantCorp today.
今天鴻巨企業有五十個人被裁員。

ord List
....
absence [ˋæbsn̩] *n.* 不在;缺席;缺勤

3.2 談論企業難題 Talking About Business Problems

❶ (Company/Business)... is in the red.
（公司／事業）負債累累。
例 The company has been in the red for years.
這家公司負債累累好幾年了。

❷ ...go on strike.
……罷工。
例 It's difficult for businesses when their workers go on strike.
員工罷工的時候，對企業而言很麻煩。

❸ (Company/Business) go bankrupt.
（公司／事業）破產。
例 An unsuccessful business might go bankrupt.
一家不成功的公司可能會破產。

❹ (Company/Business) go out of business.
（公司／事業）倒閉。
例 That company went out of business.
那家公司倒閉了。

ord List

....

go bankrupt 破產；倒閉

☹ 錯誤用法：

He had to **overwork** last week.

他上週需要加班。

☺ 正確用法：

He had to **work overtime** last week.

他上週需要加班。

::::::::: **Biz 一點通** :::::::::

Don't forget that when using <u>countable</u> nouns, such as market in the <u>singular</u> form, you need to use an <u>article</u> (a, an, or the). With words such as competition, which is actually uncountable, use "the competition," not "a competition." Similarly, we say "the pay," not "a pay." Also, <u>be aware of</u> the use of "get" with <u>past participle</u> such as fired, laid off, hired, and promoted.

不要忘了，在使用單數的可數名詞例如「market」（市場）時，你需要使用冠詞（a，an 或 the）。至於像「competition」（競爭）這類不可數的名詞，則要使用「the competition」，而不是「a competition」。同樣地，我們說「the pay」，而不是「a pay」。還有，要注意「get」與「fired」（開除）、「laid off」（裁員）、「hired」（雇用）和「promoted」（升遷）等字的連用。

 ord List

countable [ˈkaʊntəbl̩] *adj.* 可數的

singular [ˈsɪŋɡjələ] *adj.* 【文法】單數的

article [ˈɑrtɪkl̩] *n.* 【文法】冠詞

be aware of 注意……；察覺……；知道……

past participle [ˈpæst ˈpɑrtəsəpl̩] *n.* 過去分詞

4 實戰演練 Practice Exercises

I 請為下列詞語選出最適合本章的中文譯義。

❶ go on strike

(A) 打擊 (B) 罷工 (C) 打雷

❷ go bankrupt

(A) 崩盤 (B) 搶劫 (C) 破產

❸ in the red

(A) 如日中天 (B) 負債 (C) 陷入危險

II 你會如何回應下面這兩句話？

❶ Business is booming.

(A) That's great.

(B) That's too bad.

(C) Be careful.

❷ My company went bankrupt.

(A) That's good.

(B) I'm sorry to hear that.

(C) Banks are good to work for.

III 請用下列詞語寫出一篇簡短的對話。

the pay is	work overtime
the market is	there's a demand for
out of business	get hired

＊解答請見 238 頁

第 **14** 章

讓上司印象深刻與讚美同事
Impressing the Boss
And Complimenting Coworkers

Exhibiting behavior that makes a good impression at the office is not just a social nicety; it can alter your career path. If you are likeable and well thought of, then you may be considered a better candidate for promotion than someone who is unpopular or has poor people skills. Knowing the right phrases to impress people can go a long way in helping your career.

在辦公室的表現讓人留下好印象不但是社交上要注意的細節，也能夠改變你的職涯。如果你討人喜歡又給人好印象，你可能就會比不受歡迎或人際技巧欠佳的人更容易被視為拔擢的好人選。如知道使用什麼樣的詞語會給人留下好印象，對你的事業將大有助益。

1 Biz 必通句型 Need-to-Know Phrases

track 41

1.1 作出承諾 Making Promises

❶ I assure you....

我向你保證……。

例 I assure you I will improve my performance.

我向你保證我會改進我的表現。

❷ I promise....

我保證……。

例 I promise to work harder in the future.

我保證以後會更努力。

❸ I vow....

我誓言……

例 I vow to finish the project by the end of the week.

我誓言會在這週結束前完成這項專案。

❹ I pledge....

我發誓……。

例 I pledge to increase my sales record.

我發誓會提高我的銷售業績。

Word **L**ist

assure [əˈʃur] v. 向……保證；擔保

vow [vau] v. 立誓；發誓

pledge [ˈplɛdʒ] v. 宣誓；發誓

❺ I give you my word....

我向你承諾……。

例 I give you my word that it will never happen again.

我向你承諾不會再發生這樣的事了。

❻ I guarantee....

我保證……。

例 I guarantee that this <u>scheme</u> will work.

我保證這個計畫會奏效。

❼ I will ensure....

我會確保……。

例 I will ensure this assignment is done on time.

我會確保這個任務準時完成。

❽ I will make certain....

我會確保……。

例 I will make certain that the report is finished early.

我會確保這份報告提早完成。

ord List

give (sb.) one's word　（向某人）承諾

scheme [skim] *n.* 計畫；方案

1.2 讚美同事 Complimenting Coworkers

讚美表現

❶ You did a great job on....
你……做得很好。
> 例 You did a great job on that presentation.
> 你那場簡報做得很好。

❷ Nice work.
做得好。
> 例 Nice work, Joe. It was a great report.
> 做得好，喬。這份報告很不錯。

❸ Keep up the good work.
繼續保持良好的表現。
> 例 Keep up the good work, Susan.
> 繼續保持良好的表現，蘇珊。

❹ I'm impressed.
我印象非常深刻。
> 例 You're a hard worker — I'm impressed.
> 你是個努力的員工，我印象非常深刻。

Word List

impressed [ɪmˋprɛst] *adj.* 印象深刻的；深受感動的

讚美外表

❺ You look good.

你看起來很不錯。

例 You look good today, Sandra.

妳今天看起來很不錯，珊德拉。

❻ You look sharp.

你看起來很帥／時髦。

例 You look sharp in that suit, Charles.

你穿那套西裝看起來很帥，查爾斯。

❼ Nice outfit.

衣服很好看。

例 Nice outfit, Terry. It's very pretty.

衣服很好看，泰利。非常漂亮。

❽ Nice hairdo.

髮型很好看。

例 Nice hairdo, Wendy. Which hair salon do you go to?

髮型很好看，溫蒂。妳都上哪一間髮廊？

 ord List

sharp [ʃɑrp] *adj.* （裝扮）時髦的；帥氣的

outfit [ˋaʊt͵fɪt] *n.* （為特定目的而穿的）服裝

hairdo [ˋhɛr͵du] *n.* 髮型

salon [səˋlɑn] *n.* （時髦的）美容院

2 實戰會話 Show Time

2.1 讓上司印象深刻 Impressing the Boss

 track 42

Darren has invited his supervisor, Simon, to lunch. This time, Darren isn't going to apologize. Instead, he's decided to make a good impression by making promises to Simon that he will improve his performance.

Darren: Simon, I want to take this opportunity to say that I give you my word that my performance with the company will improve.

Simon: That's great to hear, Darren.

Darren: The next time I'm given an important assignment, I promise I won't let you down. I will ensure that everything is done right and on time.

Simon: I must say, Darren, I like your attitude. I'm impressed with it.

Darren: That's very nice of you. I appreciate it. By the way, I like your suit — you look sharp.

Simon: You're too kind. You know, if you want to prove yourself to the company, I do have another assignment for you. It would mean working overtime quite a bit, however.

Darren: That's not a problem. If you give me the assignment, I'll make certain I don't make any mistakes. You can rely on me.

Simon: Great. That's what I like to hear.

Darren: You can count on me.

譯 文

達倫邀請了他的主管賽門去吃午飯。這一次，達倫不打算道歉，相反地；他決定向賽門保證他會改進自己的表現，好讓賽門留下好印象。

達倫：　賽門，我想利用這個機會跟你說，我向你承諾我在公司的表現會有所改進。

賽門：　我很高興聽你這麼說，達倫。

達倫：　下一次我被分到重要的任務時，我保證不會讓你失望。我會確保每件事都會準時並且正確無誤地完成。

賽門：　我必須說，達倫，我喜歡你的態度。我對它印象非常深刻。

達倫：　你人真好，我很感激。對了，我很喜歡你的西裝，你看起來很帥。

賽門：　你太客氣了。你知道嗎，如果你想向公司證明自己的能力，我倒有另一項任務給你。不過那表示你得加不少班。

達倫：　那不成問題。如果你把這個任務交給我，我會確保自己不會犯下任何錯誤。你可以信賴我。

賽門：　好極了，我就想聽你這麼說。

達倫：　你可以依賴我。

ord List

make a good impression　留下好印象
make promises to sb.　向某人承諾……；答應某人……
rely on sb.　信賴某人
count on sb.　依賴某人；指望某人

2.2 讚美同事 Complimenting Coworkers

After his lunch meeting with Simon, Darren <u>is in a good mood</u>.

Darren: Hi, Brenda. Nice outfit. You look good!

Brenda: Thanks very much, Darren.

Darren: Nice hairdo, too. Oh, I forgot to mention that you did a great job on that last assignment.

Brenda: Thanks, I appreciate it.

Darren: Also, I think I was a bit rude to you before. I guarantee I won't do it again.

Paul <u>strides</u> by <u>with a spring in his step</u> and a new briefcase in his hand.

Paul: Hi Brenda. You look good today.

Brenda: That's very nice of you, thanks. You look sharp, too.

Darren: Hi Paul. Hey, I heard you made the most sales again this month. Nice work. Keep up the good work.

Paul: Thanks. I saw you and Simon having lunch. What were you two talking about?

Darren: I vowed to do a better job at WHT in the future. I pledged that I wouldn't make any more big mistakes.

Paul: That sounds like a really smart thing to do.

Darren: Thanks very much.

譯 文

在和賽門的午餐會後，達倫心情很好。

達倫：　嗨，布蘭達。衣服很好看。妳看起來很不錯！

布蘭達：多謝啦，達倫。

達倫：　髮型也很好看。噢，我忘了說，妳上次那個任務做得很好。

布蘭達：謝謝，我很感激。

達倫：　還有，我想我之前對妳有點粗魯。我保證不會再這樣了。

保羅腳步輕快地大步走過，手上拎著一個新的公事包。

保羅：　嗨，布蘭達。妳今天看起來很不錯。

布蘭達：你人真好，謝謝。你看起來也很帥。

達倫：　嗨，保羅。嘿，我聽說你這個月又創下最高銷售量。做得好，繼續保持良好的表現。

保羅：　謝謝。我看到你和賽門一起吃午飯。你們兩個談了些什麼？

達倫：　我誓言以後要在 WHT 表現得更好。我還發誓不會再犯更多大錯。

保羅：　聽起來像是非常聰明的作法。

達倫：　多謝。

ord List

be in a good mood 心情很好
stride [straɪd] *v.* 跨大步走
with a spring in one's step 腳步輕盈（spring [sprɪŋ] *n.* 跳躍）

3 Biz 加分句型 Nice-to-Know Phrases

track 43

3.1 更多作承諾的片語
More Phrases for Promising

❶ You can count on me.
你可以依賴我。
例 I'll finish it by 6 p.m. today. You can count on me.
我會在今天下午六點前完成它的。你可以依賴我。

❷ You can rely on me.
你可以信賴我。
例 You can rely on me to do a good job.
你可以信賴我會有好表現。

❸ I won't fail.
我不會失敗的。
例 Don't worry, Brendan — I won't fail.
別擔心,布蘭登,我不會失敗的。

❹ I won't let you down.
我不會讓你失望的。
例 I won't let you down, Fred.
我不會讓你失望的,佛瑞德。

3.2 接受讚美 Accepting a Compliment

❶ I appreciate it.
我很感激。
例 Thanks, I appreciate it.
　　謝謝，我很感激。

❷ That's very nice of you.
你人真好。
例 That's very nice of you to say that.
　　你那麼說真好心。

❸ Thanks very much.
多謝。
例 Thanks very much — I appreciate it.
　　多謝，我很感激。

❹ You're too kind.
你太客氣了。
例 You're too kind, Veronica.
　　妳太客氣了，維若妮卡。

┌──────────── 小心陷阱 ────────────┐

☹ 錯誤用法：

Keep the good work.

繼續保持好表現。

☺ 正確用法：

Keep up the good work.

繼續保持好表現。

└─────────────────────────────────┘

┌──────────── Biz 一點通 ────────────┐

When making promises and giving compliments, it is important to be sincere. Don't <u>overdo</u> it. If people <u>suspect</u> that you are <u>insincere</u>, then they will probably not believe you and most likely not trust you. Engaging in too much <u>flattery</u> with the boss may also earn you the very <u>unflattering</u> nickname "<u>brown-noser</u>," or "<u>ass-kisser</u>."

在作承諾和給予讚美時，真誠是很重要的；不要太過火。如果別人懷疑你不真誠，他們可能會不相信你，而且非常可能會不信任你。過度奉承上司也會為你換來非常不討好的綽號，如「狗腿」或「馬屁精」。

└─────────────────────────────────┘

Ｗord List

overdo [ˌovəˋdu] *v.* 做得過火；做得過度

suspect [səˋspɛkt] *v.* 懷疑……；認為……可疑

insincere [ˌɪnsɪnˋsɪr] *adj.* 無誠意的；不誠實的

flattery [ˋflætərɪ] *n.* 諂媚；奉承

unflattering [ʌnˋflætərɪŋ] *adj.* 不奉承的；不討好的

brown-noser [ˋbraʊnˌnozə] *n.*【俚】奉承別人的人

ass-kisser [ˋæsˌkɪsə] *n.*【卑】馬屁精

4　實戰演練 Practice Exercises

I　請為下列詞語選出最適合本章的中文譯義。

❶ I give you my word.

(A) 我對你食言。　(B) 我送你一句話。　(C) 我向你承諾。

❷ go a long way

(A) 走很久的路　(B) 很有助益　(C) 繞遠路

❸ people skills

(A) 生育方法　(B) 人工智慧　(C) 人際技巧

II　你會如何回應下面這兩句話？

❶ I'll ensure that I will do a good job.

(A) No, I'm not sure.

(B) Yes, it's a good job.

(C) That's good.

❷ I appreciate it.

(A) You're welcome.

(B) Nice work.

(C) You're too kind.

III　請用下列詞語寫出一篇簡短的對話。

I promise.	I give you my word.
I'll ensure	I'm impressed.
You can count on me.	You look good.

＊解答請見 239 頁

辦公室八卦
Office Gossip

Like it or not, gossip is an inevitable part of office life. Indeed, many people actually thrive on gossiping about their coworkers and friends and hearing about gossip from others. Is it caused by boredom or human nature? Whatever the case, here are some common phrases that will allow you to participate in this popular office activity. One word of caution, though: Be careful who's listening!

不管你喜不喜歡，八卦都是辦公室生活無法避免的一部分。的確，事實上許多人熱愛講他們同事和朋友的八卦，也喜歡聽別人講八卦消息。這是因為無聊還是人性？不管是哪一種原因，下面這些常用的詞語，可以讓你參與這種非常普遍的辦公室活動。不過，要提醒你小心：注意是誰在聽！

1 Biz 必通句型 Need-to-Know Phrases

 track 44

1.1 提起八卦話題 Introducing Gossip

分享八卦

❶ I heard from someone that....

我聽某人說……。

例 I heard from someone that Sam and his wife are getting a divorce.

我聽某人說山姆和他太太要離婚了。

❷ Listen to what I've heard....

聽聽我聽說了什麼……。

例 Listen to what I've heard — the company is going to downsize.

聽聽我聽說了什麼──公司要縮編了。

❸ Do you want to know a secret?

你想知道一個秘密嗎？

例 Do you want to know a secret? Candy is having an affair with Larry.

你想知道一個秘密嗎？甘蒂和賴瑞有染。

❹ Guess what?

你猜怎樣？

例 Guess what? George is gay.

你猜怎樣？喬治是同性戀。

Word List

gossip ［ˋgɑsəp］ *n./v.* 八卦／談論他人的八卦

get a divorce 離婚

downsize ［ˋdaʊn͵saɪz］ *v.* 裁減（員工）人數

have an affair with sb. 與……有染；與……有不正常關係

gay [ge] *n./adj.*【口語】同性戀者／同性戀的

詢問誰有八卦

❺What's new?

有什麼新鮮事？

例 Hi Mike. What's new?

　　嗨，麥克。有什麼新鮮事？

❻What's up?

有什麼消息？

例 What's up, Nancy?

　　有什麼消息，南西？

❼Do you have any good gossip?

你有什麼精采的八卦嗎？

例 Do you have any good gossip today, Linda?

　　妳今天有什麼精采的八卦嗎，琳達？

❽Any news about...?

有任何關於……的消息嗎？

例 Any news about the new sales person?

　　有任何關於那個新業務員的消息嗎？

1.2 回應八卦 Responding to Gossip

表現驚訝和懷疑

❶ That's <u>incredible</u>.（驚訝）

太不可思議了。

例 Robert is quitting the company? That's incredible.

羅勃要離開公司？太不可思議了。

❷ That's <u>unbelievable</u>.（驚訝）

真令人難以相信。

例 That's unbelievable. I didn't know Jim got fired.

真令人難以相信。我不知道吉姆被開除了。

❸ I can't believe it.（驚訝或懷疑）

我真不敢相信。

例 Randy and Gordon got into a fight yesterday? I can't believe it.

蘭迪和戈登昨天打起來了？我真不敢相信。

❹ No way!（懷疑）

不可能！

例 You think Grace will be promoted to marketing manager? No way!

你覺得葛莉絲會被升為行銷經理？不可能！

Word List

incredible [ɪn`krɛdəbl] *adj.* 不可思議的

unbelievable [ˌʌnbə`livəbl] *adj.* 難以置信的

表示相信

❺It doesn't surprise me....

我並不驚訝……。

例 It doesn't surprise me that the company is going to lay off several people.

公司要裁掉幾個人我並不驚訝。

❻It's not hard to believe....

這不難相信……。

例 Pete <u>split up with</u> Vicky? It's not hard to believe.

彼特和維琪分手了？這不難相信。

❼I don't doubt....（強烈）

我毫不懷疑……。

例 I don't doubt that Debbie will get fired.

我毫不懷疑黛比會被開除。

❽I knew it!（更強烈）

我就知道！

例 Laura is <u>going out with Ralph</u>? I knew it!

蘿拉在和羅大約會？我就知道！

ord List

split up with sb. 和某人分手
go out with sb. 與……約會

2 實戰會話 Show Time

track 45

2.1 在派對八卦 Gossiping at a Party

A week ago, Darren moved into a new apartment. To cele-brate, he has invited many of his WHT coworkers over to his place tonight. Away from the office, the employees are eager to engage in gossip about the people who aren't at the party.

Laura: Does anyone have any good gossip?

Sandra: I've heard from someone that Paul and Brenda are going out with each other.

Darren: What? I can't believe it. Is that really true?

Sandra: Steve saw them kissing each other a few days ago.

Laura: I knew it! I thought they were more than just friends.

Darren: That's incredible. Paul told me I shouldn't have an office romance with Brenda because it's too difficult.

Laura: It doesn't surprise me he told you that. He wanted Brenda for himself. I've got some more gossip. Listen to what I've heard: Paul is quitting WHT.

Darren: No way! He's the company's top salesman and sales manager. Where did you hear that?

Laura: I heard Simon mention it to someone. He's going to a company called Sky-High Engineering.

Sandra: I can't believe it!

Darren: Why not?

Sandra: Paul told me that company was in the red and would probably go out of business. <u>What a liar!</u>

Darren: That guy really makes me mad.

譯文

一個星期前，達倫搬進了一間新公寓。為了慶祝，他邀請了許多 WHT 的同事今晚到他家來。遠離辦公室，員工們都急欲說說沒來派對的人的八卦。

蘿拉：　誰有什麼精采的八卦嗎？

珊德拉：我聽某人說保羅和布蘭達在約會。

達倫：　什麼？我真不敢相信。這是真的嗎？

珊德拉：史提夫幾天前看到他們在接吻。

蘿拉：　我就知道！我就覺得他們不只是朋友。

達倫：　太不可思議了。保羅跟我說我不應和布蘭達談辦公室戀情，因為這樣太麻煩了。

蘿拉：　我並不驚訝他那樣跟你說；他想要獨占布蘭達。我還有更多的八卦。聽聽我聽說了什麼：保羅要離開 WHT 了。

達倫：　不可能！他是公司最頂尖的業務員，又是業務經理。妳從哪裡聽來的？

蘿拉：　我聽到賽門跟某個人提起這件事。他要去一家叫天高工程的公司。

珊德拉：我真不敢相信！

達倫：　為什麼？

珊德拉：保羅告訴我那家公司負債累累，而且可能會倒閉。真是個大騙子！

達倫：　那傢伙真的讓我很生氣。

ord List

What a liar！真是個大騙子！

2.2 更多辦公室八卦 More Office Gossip

It's another Monday morning and our WHT employees are taking their break in the <u>corridor</u>. Paul is still the hot topic of conversation.

Laura: Do you want to know a secret?

Sandra: Sure. What's up? Any news about Paul?

Laura: I just saw Paul wearing sunglasses in the office. I think he has a black eye.

Sandra: That's incredible. I wonder if Darren hit him?

Laura: Probably. I think Darren was pretty mad at him.

Steve enters the corridor <u>chewing</u> on a donut and <u>lights up</u> a cigarette.

Sandra: Hi Steve.

Steve: Hi Sandra. Hi Laura. What's new?

Laura: Darren hit Paul, and now Paul has a black eye.

Steve: I can't believe that! Are you sure?

Sandra: Paul is wearing sunglasses, and Darren was mad at Paul.

Steve: But are you one hundred percent sure that it was Darren who hit Paul? Who told you that?

Laura: Well, no one told us. It does <u>make a lot of sense</u>, though.

Steve: Maybe he got into a fight at a bar. Paul does like to drink and he <u>has a temper</u>.

Laura: It's not hard to believe. Wait. Here's Paul now. Let's ask him.

Sandra: Hi, Paul. Nice sunglasses. I heard from someone that you got into a fight.

Paul: No way! Who says? No. The reason I'm wearing sunglasses is that I had <u>laser</u> eye <u>surgery</u> on the weekend and my eyes are a little <u>sensitive</u> to light right now.

Sandra: Oh, sorry. I guess I heard wrong.

譯 文

又是星期一早晨，我們的 WHT 員工正在走廊上休息，保羅仍舊是談話中的熱門話題。

蘿拉： 妳想知道一個秘密嗎？

珊德拉：當然。有什麼消息？有任何關於保羅的消息嗎？

蘿拉： 我剛看到保羅在辦公室裡戴著墨鏡。我想他一隻眼睛被打黑了。

珊德拉：太不可思議了。不曉得是不是達倫打的？

蘿拉： 有可能。我想達倫真的很氣他。

史提夫走進走廊，一邊嚼著甜甜圈，一邊點燃一支香菸。

珊德拉：嗨，史提夫。

史提夫：嗨，珊德拉。嗨，蘿拉。有什麼新鮮事？

蘿拉： 達倫打了保羅，現在保羅臉上有個黑眼圈。

史提夫：我真不敢相信！妳確定嗎？

珊德拉：保羅戴著太陽眼鏡，而且達倫之前很氣保羅。

史提夫：但是妳百分之百確定打保羅的是達倫嗎？是誰告訴妳們的？

蘿拉： 嗯，沒人告訴我們，不過這的確很合理。

史提夫：也許他在酒吧和人打架。保羅的確很喜歡喝一杯，而且他脾氣也不好。

蘿拉： 這不難相信。等一下，保羅來了，我們問問他。

珊德拉：嗨，保羅，太陽眼鏡很不錯。我聽某人說你和人打架了。

保羅： 不可能！誰說的？才不是。我之所以戴太陽眼鏡是因為我週末去動眼睛雷射手術，我的眼睛現在有點畏光。

珊德拉：噢，抱歉。我想是我聽錯了。

Word List

corridor [ˈkɔrədə] *n.* 走廊；通道

chew [tʃu] *v.* 咀嚼

light up 【口語】 點燃

make sense 合理

have a temper 【口語】 脾氣暴躁

laser [ˈlezə] *n.* 雷射

surgery [ˈsɝdʒərɪ] *n.* （外科的）手術

sensitive [ˈsɛnsətɪv] *adj.* 對……敏感的

3 Biz 加分句型 Nice-to-Know Phrases

 track 46

3.1 詢問八卦 Gossiping — Questioning

❶ Is that really true?
此事當真？
例 Alicia got a divorce yesterday? Is that really true?
艾莉西亞昨天離婚了？此事當真？

❷ Are you sure (sth.)?
你確定（某件事）嗎？
例 Are you sure the company is being sold?
你確定公司要被賣掉嗎？

❸ Is that for certain?
此事確定嗎？
例 You said we're not getting a bonus this year. Is that for certain?
你說我們今年不會有紅利。此事確定嗎？

❹ Are you one hundred percent sure (sth.)?
你百分之百確定（某件事）嗎？
例 Are you one hundred percent sure that we have to work overtime for the whole week?
你百分之百確定我們整個週末都必須加班嗎？

3.2 查證八卦來源 Gossiping — Checking the Source

❶ How do you know that (sth.)?
你怎麼知道（某件事）？
例 How do you know that the staff party is cancelled?
你怎麼知道員工派對被取消了？

❷ Where did you hear that (sth.)?
你從哪裡聽來（某件事）的？
例 Where did you hear that I'm quitting the company?
你從哪裡聽來我要離開公司的？

❸ Who told you (sth.)?
是誰告訴你（某件事）？
例 Who told you that the boss hates Sandy?
是誰告訴你老闆討厭珊蒂的？

❹ Who says (sth.)?
誰說（某件事）？
例 Who says Brent is a bad worker?
誰說布藍特是個差勁的員工？

::::::::: 小心陷阱 :::::::::

☹ 錯誤用法：

Does anyone **get** any good gossip?

誰有什麼精采的八卦嗎？

☺ 正確用法：

Does anyone **have** any good gossip?

誰有什麼精采的八卦嗎？

::::::::: Biz 一點通 :::::::::

Just as it is <u>crucial</u> to be careful about who the subject of your gossip is, it is also important to be <u>cautious</u> about who you share gossip with, i.e., the person to whom you speak. Spreading <u>erroneous</u> <u>rumors</u> can come back to <u>haunt</u> you, even if you just repeated some gossip another person passed on to you. If a coworker finds out you are saying false things behind his or her back, then there may be <u>repercussions</u>, especially if that person <u>holds a position of authority</u>.

正如小心你八卦的主角是誰非常重要，留意你和誰分享八卦也同樣重要；也就是說，要注意和你講話的人是誰。散布錯誤的謠言很可能會回過頭纏擾你，就算你只是重複一些另一個人傳達給你的八卦。如果一個同事發現你在他或她的背後說一些不實的事情，那麼就可能會有不良的影響，特別是如果這個人位高權重的話。

ord List

cruical [ˋkruʃəl] *adj.* 決定性的；極重要的

cautious [ˋkɔʃəs] *adj.* 小心的；謹慎的

erroneous [əˋronɪəs] *adj.* 【文語】錯誤的

rumor [ˋrumə] *n.* 傳聞；謠言

haunt [hɔnt] *v.* 纏擾

repercussion [ˌripəˋkʌʃən] *n.*（事情、事件的）反響

hold a position of authority 位高權重

4 實戰演練 Practice Exercises

Ⅰ 請為下列詞語選出最適合本章的中文譯義。

❶ have an affair with

(A) 與……有關係 (B) 與……有染 (C) 與……共事

❷ hold a position of authority

(A) 處事公正 (B) 身為權威人士 (C) 位高權重

❸ have a temper

(A) 脾氣暴躁 (B) 發高燒 (C) 性情溫和

Ⅱ 你會如何回應下面這兩句話？

❶ Do you want to know a secret?

(A) I don't know any secrets.

(B) OK, sure.

(C) I can't believe it.

❷ No way!

(A) Where did you hear that?

(B) I'm sorry.

(C) Yes, it's true.

Ⅲ 請用下列詞語寫出一篇簡短的對話。

I heard from someone that	What's up?
I can't believe it.	It doesn't surprise me.
Who told you?	Is that for certain?

＊解答請見 240 頁

第 **16** 章

談論目標與未來計畫
Talking About Goals and Future Plans

Setting goals can be a difficult and complicated process. Even more challenging is conveying these objectives in a language that is not your native one. Yet, in the workplace, having — and being able to communicate — clear goals and plans for the future is considered a very valuable trait. This chapter is devoted to helping you achieve the goal of effectively discussing your goals and asking others about their plans for the future.

設定目標可能會是個困難而複雜的過程,更困難的是要用不是你母語的語言來傳達這些目標。但是,在職場中,有清楚的未來目標和計畫又能將它們傳達出來,被視為一項非常寶貴的特質。本章即專為幫助你達成有效討論你的目標並詢問他人未來計畫這個目標而設計。

1 Biz 必通句型 Need-to-Know Phrases

 track 47

1.1 討論目標 Discussing Goals

目標較薄弱或不明確時

❶ I hope to....

我希望……。

例 I hope to get an MBA in the next few years.

我希望能在接下來幾年內取得企管碩士學位。

❷ My wish is to....

我的希望是……。

例 My wish is to continue to get promotions.

我的希望是繼續不斷獲得升遷。

❸ My <u>desire</u> is to....

我的願望是……。

例 My desire is to own a big house someday.

我的願望是有一天能擁有一間大房子。

❹ I have a dream to....

我有個夢想希望能……。

例 I have a dream to start my own company.

我有個夢想希望能創辦自己的公司。

 Word List

desire [dɪˋzaɪr] *n.* 渴望；慾望；願望

目標較強烈或肯定時

❺ My <u>vision</u> is to....

我的願景是……。

例 My vision is to become <u>head</u> of the department.

我的願景是成為部門主管。

❻ My goal is to....

我的目標是……。

例 My goal is to keep <u>advancing</u> within the company.

我的目標是在公司裡持續晉升。

❼ I plan to....

我計畫……。

例 I plan to go to university next year.

我計畫明年去上大學。

❽ I am going to.... / I will....

我要……。／我會……。

例 I am going to open a restaurant.

我要開一家餐廳。

ord List

vision [ˋvɪʒən] *n.* 對未來的洞察力；願景

head [hɛd] *n.* （權力、統轄的）主管；領袖；長官

advance [ədˋvæns] *v.* 晉升

1.2 詢問他人的目標 Asking About Someone's Goals

❶ What are your future goals?
你未來的目標是什麼？
例 Tell me, John. What are your future goals?
告訴我，約翰，你未來的目標是什麼？

❷ What are your plans for the future?
你未來的計畫是什麼？
例 Tina, what are your plans for the future with this company?
提娜，妳在這家公司未來的計畫是什麼？

❸ Where do you want to be in (time)?
你在（時間）後想要達成什麼目標？
例 Where do you want to be in five years, Stephanie?
妳在五年後後想要達成什麼目標，史蒂芬妮？

❹ What do you see yourself doing (time phrase)?
你認為自己在（一段時間）後會有什麼成就？
例 What do you see yourself doing after a few years in your position?
你認為自己在這個職位待幾年後會有什麼成就？

❺ Have you thought much about your future?

你有沒有好好想過自己的未來？

例 Paul, have you thought much about your future? What do you want to do?

保羅，你有沒有好好想過自己的未來？你想做什麼？

❻ Have you <u>set any goals</u>?

你有沒有設立任何目標？

例 Have you set any goals for the future, Ian?

你有沒有為未來設立任何目標，伊安？

❼ What do you hope to <u>accomplish</u> <u>in the short term</u>?

你在短期內希望達成些什麼？

例 Let me ask you, Evelyn — what do you hope to accomplish in the short-term?

我問問妳，艾芙琳，妳在短期內希望達成些什麼？

❽ What would you like to do <u>in the long run</u>?

你最終想要做什麼？

例 What would you like to do in the long run, Vince? Have you ever thought about that?

你最終想要做什麼，文斯？你有沒有想過這個問題？

 ord List

set a goal 設立目標

accomplish [ə`kɑmplɪʃ] v. 完成；達成

in the short term 短期內

in the long run 終究；最後

2 實戰會話 Show Time

2.1 表現成績考核（1）
The Performance Review I

track 48

Now that Darren has been working at WHT for three months, his probationary period has ended. WHT's personnel manager, Amanda Sharp, has called Darren into her office for a discussion.

Amanda: Darren, please sit down. I'd like to talk to you about your last three months at WHT. First, let's talk about your accomplishments.

Darren: Sure. I believe my achievements include working hard every day, completing many assignments, and learning a lot on the job. I have <u>attained</u> many goals in the last three months.

Amanda: Yes, I see that Steve has given you a very good performance <u>rating</u>. Good work. However, I also notice that you had some problems with the designs for the German project.

Darren: That's true. However, since that <u>incident</u>, I have <u>made a lot of progress</u> in learning more about the application process. My goal is to never make another mistake at WHT ever again.

Amanda: Darren, I'm sorry, but that's not <u>realistic</u>. Everyone makes mistakes occasionally. The important thing is to learn from your mistakes and not repeat them.

Darren: I guess you're right. I should say that my wish is to make as few mistakes as possible.

如今達倫已經在 WHT 工作了三個月，他的試用期已經滿了。 WHT 的人事部經理艾曼達‧夏普把達倫叫進她辦公室要跟他談一談。

艾曼達：達倫，請坐。我想和你談談你過去三個月在 WHT 的表現。首先，我們來談談你的成就。

達倫：　好。我認為我的成就包括每天努力工作、完成多項任務，以及在工作上學到許多東西。我在過去三個月裡達成了許多目標。

艾曼達：沒錯，我看到史提夫對你的表現給了很不錯的評價。做得不錯。不過，我也注意到你在德國專案的設計圖上出了一點問題。

達倫：　沒錯。不過，自從那個事件之後，我在了解申請過程上有很大的進展。我的目標是絕不在 WHT 犯下另一個錯誤。

艾曼達：達倫，抱歉，但是那是不切實際的。每個人偶而都會犯錯，重要的是要從你的錯誤中學習，不要重蹈覆轍。

達倫：　我想妳說得對，我應該說我的希望是儘量少犯錯。

Word List

attain [əˋten] *v.* 達到

rating [ˋretɪŋ] *n.* 評價；核定等級

incident [ˋɪnsədn̩t] *n.* 事件

make progress 進步；進展

realistic [͵rɪəˋlɪstɪk] *adj.* 現實的；實際的

2.2 表現成績考核（2）— 談論未來計畫
The Performance Review II — Talking About Future Plans

After a long and <u>dramatic</u> <u>pause</u>, Amanda <u>folds her arms</u> and <u>leans</u> forward in her chair.

Amanda: Darren, I want to let you know that, despite some problems that you've had, everyone feels that you have done a good job over the past three months. In other words, you've passed probation. Congratulations!

Darren: That's great. Thanks. I was a little worried.

Amanda: I understand. Now, I want to talk about your future with the company. Have you thought much about your future at WHT? Have you set any goals?

Darren: Yes. I hope to work hard and earn promotions over time. My desire is to have a good career within the company.

Amanda: That sounds great. What do you see yourself doing in five years? Where do you want to be at that time?

Darren: Actually, I have a dream to be the head of a department, and to have a lot of responsibility. I plan to go to night school and earn a Master's degree.

Amanda: Wonderful. What would you like to accomplish in the short term at WHT?

Darren: My vision is to keep working hard and earn the respect and confidence from my <u>supervisors</u>, and to keep learning as much as I can.

Amanda: That's great, Darren. I'm sure you'll have a good career here at WHT.

在一段長久、戲劇性的沉默之後，艾曼達交疊雙臂，坐在她的椅子上，身體向前傾。

艾曼達：達倫，我要你知道，雖然你曾經有過一些問題，但是每個人都覺得你過去三個來表現得很好。換句話說，你已經通過了試用期，恭喜！

達倫：　好極了，謝謝。我原先還有點擔心。

艾曼達：我了解。現在，我要和你談談你在公司的未來。你有沒有好好想過自己在 WHT 的未來？你有沒有設立任何目標？

達倫：　有。我希望能努力工作，並適時獲得升遷。我的願望是在公司裡有個很好的事業。

艾曼達：聽起來很棒。你認為自己在五年後會有什麼成就？到那時候想要達成什麼目標？

達倫：　事實上，我有個夢想希望能成為部門主管，肩負許多責任。我計畫要去上夜間部取得碩士學位。

艾曼達：好極了。你在 WHT 短期內想要達成些什麼？

達倫：　我的願景是繼續努力工作，贏得主管們的尊重與信心，並繼續盡可能地學習。

艾曼達：太好了，達倫，我確定你在 WHT 會有一個很不錯的事業。

ord List

dramatic [drə`mætɪk] *adj.* 戲劇性的

pause [pɔs] *n.* 停頓；暫停

fold one's arms 交叉雙臂（fold [fod] *v.* 交疊）

lean [lin] *v.* 傾身；屈身

supervisor [ˌsupə`vaɪzə] *n.* 管理人；監督者

3 Biz 加分句型 Nice-to-Know Phrases

 track 49

3.1 談論成就
Talking About Accomplishments

❶ My achievements include....

我的成就包括……。

例 My achievements include being sales manager for five years and helping the company grow.

我的成就包括身任業務經理五年以及幫助公司成長。

❷ My accomplishments are....

我的成就是……。

例 My accomplishments this year are attracting several new clients, increasing sales, and gaining more product knowledge.

我今年的成就是爭取到幾位新客戶、提高銷售業績以及獲得更多產品的知識。

❸ I have attained....

我已經達成了……。

例 I have attained many goals so far.

我目前已經達成了許多目標。

❹ I've made (a lot of) progress....

我……有進步（許多）。

例 I've made progress in many areas.

我在許多方面都有進步。

3.2　評論他人的目標 Commenting on Someone's Goals

正面

❶ That sounds great.（用於評論目標）

聽起來很棒。

例 You plan to get your MBA? That sounds great.

你計畫要取得企管碩士學位？聽起來很棒。

❷ Good work.（用於評論成就）

做得不錯。

例 Good work for accomplishing so much!

你獲得這麼多成就，做得不錯！

負面

❸ That's unrealistic.

那是不切實際的。

例 You want to be president of the company in two years? That's unrealistic, Barney.

你想在兩年內成為公司的總裁？那是不切實際的，巴尼。

❹ That's (just) unachievable.

那（根本）是不可能達成的。

例 You want to make a million dollars next year? I'm sorry, Harriet, that's unachievable.

妳想在明年賺進一百萬？對不起，哈莉葉，那是不可能達成的。

ord List

unachievable [ʌnəˋtʃivəbl] *adj.* 不可能達成的

::::::::: 小心陷阱 :::::::::

☹ 錯誤用法：

I will get an MBA **after** two years.

我會在兩年內取得企管碩士學位。

☺ 正確用法：

I will get an MBA **in** two years.

我會在兩年內取得企管碩士學位。

::::::::: Biz 一點通 :::::::::

The differences in the language of talking about goals can <u>be</u> <u>subtle</u>, but there is a <u>distinct</u> and noticeable difference in how things are phrased. Using terms such as "I hope," "My wish is," or "I have a dream to," conveys to the listener that your goals are somewhat uncertain and that you haven't made <u>specific</u> plans in particular areas. On the other hand, phrases like "I plan," "My goal," "I am going to," and "I will," are more <u>definite</u> and indicate that you have already done some serious thinking about your future.

談論目標時的語言差異可能很細微，但是如何措辭卻有明確、清楚的差別。使用「我希望」、「我的希望是」或「我的夢想希望能」這類詞語，向聽者傳達出的是你的目標還有些不確定，你還沒有在特定的方面作出明確的計畫。相對地，像「我計畫」、「我的目標」、「我要」和「我會」這類的詞語則比較明確，意味著你已經認真地思考過你的未來。

ord List

subtle [ˋsʌtl] *adj.* 細微的；微妙的

distinct [dɪˋstɪŋkt] *adj.* 明顯的；清楚的

specific [spɪˋsɪfɪk] *adj.* 明確的；特定的

definite [ˋdɛfənɪt] *adj.* 明確的；確定的

4 實戰演練 Practice Exercises

I 請為下列詞語選出最適合本章的中文譯義。

❶ My vision is to...

(A) 我幻想去…… (B) 我察覺到…… (C) 我的願景是……

❷ set a goal

(A) 命中目標 (B) 設立目標 (C) 得分

❸ in the log run

(A) 進行長跑比賽 (B) 終究 (C) 逃亡很久

II 你會如何回應下面這兩句話？

❶ I have a dream of being a doctor.

(A) I sleep well.

(B) That sounds great.

(C) Good work.

❷ What are your plans for the future?

(A) I'm going to the dentist tomorrow.

(B) I'm going to be a dentist.

(C) My accomplishments include being a dentist.

III 請用下列詞語寫出一篇簡短的對話。

My goal	I'm going to
What are your future goals?	I hope to
Where do you want to be?	That sounds great.

＊解答請見 241 頁

實戰演練
Answer Keys

Chapter 1 和同事初次見面與問候

I 1. (A) 2. (C) 3. (B)

II 1. (B) 2. (A)

❶ 很高興你能加入公司。

(A) 是的，這家公司不錯。

(B) 謝謝。

(C) 我也很高興認識你。

❷ 我給你我的名片好嗎？

(A) 當然好，謝謝。

(B) 在這裡。

(C) 抱歉，我沒有名片。

III 範例解答

Tony: Sally, I'd like you to meet Ben. Ben is new to the company.

Sally: Hi Ben. It's good to have you in the company. I'm in sales. I'm responsible for sales to North America.

Ben: It's nice to meet you, Sally. Do you have a card?

Sally: Yes. Here you are.

東尼：莎莉，我介紹班給妳認識。班是公司的新進人員。

莎莉：嗨，班，很高興你能加入公司。我在業務部，負責北美的業務。

班 ：很高興認識妳，莎莉。妳有名片嗎？

莎莉：有，喏。

規劃安排

I　1. (C)　2. (B)　3. (C)

II　1. (B)　2. (A)

❶ 你何時比較方便？

(A) 我正在忙。

(B) 我星期三早上可以。

(C) 應該沒問題。

❷ 我們可不可以改約另一個時間？

(A) 當然，沒問題。

(B) 現在時間是早上十一點。

(C) 好極了，那我們到時見。

III 範例解答

Fred: Sarah, what is your schedule like on Friday? Do you have any free time on that day?

Sarah: Yes, I think so.

Fred: OK, why don't we make it 3:30 p.m.?

Sarah: That sounds fine. Oh, wait, I didn't realize that I have another appointment at that time. Why don't we make it Thursday morning at 10 o'clock?

Fred: No problem. So that's Thursday at 10 a.m., right?

Sarah: Right, see you then!

佛萊德：莎拉，妳星期五的時間是如何安排的？妳那天有沒有空？

莎拉　：有，我想應該有。

佛萊德：好，那我們何不約在下午三點半？

莎拉　：應該沒問題。啊，等一下，我之前沒想到我那個時候有另外一個約，我們何不訂在星期四早上十點？

佛萊德：沒問題。所以是星期四早上十點，對吧？

莎拉　：沒錯，到時見！

Chapter
3 談論專案與任務

Ⅰ 1. (B) 2. (C) 3. (C)

Ⅱ 1. (C) 2. (B)

❶我們這項專案的進度落後。

　(A) 好極了。

　(B) 不，是在專案的前面。

　(C) 我們想個辦法加快速度吧。

❷早點開始工作也許是個好主意。

　(A) 八點時。

　(B) 謝謝你的建議。

　(C) 我沒有任何主意。

Ⅲ 範例解答

Sonia: Gordon, the deadline for the project is next Wednesday. I suggest we discuss it tomorrow morning.

Gordon:That's a great idea, Sonia. Will you take care of calling everyone?

Sonia: Sure. In my opinion, most of the work must be done before the end of Monday.

桑妮亞：戈登，專案的最後期限是下星期三。我建議我們明天早上討論一下。

戈登　：好主意，桑妮亞。妳能負責打電話給大家嗎？

桑妮亞：當然。依我看，大部分的工作必須在星期一結束前完成。

Chapter 4 與人閒聊

I 1. (C) 2. (A) 3. (B)

II 1. (A) 2. (B)

❶ 最近工作如何？

(A) 還不錯，謝謝。

(B) 我搭公車。

(C) 我十分樂意。

❷ 你通常何時去吃午飯？

(A) 我昨天十二點半去吃午飯。

(B) 中午十二點。

(C) 沒有，我還沒吃午飯。

III 範例解答

Tim:　Hi, Sally. Did you hear we're getting a bonus this year?

Sally:　That's great. Do you know how much it will be?

Tim:　Not really. Hey, how was your weekend?

Sally:　Not very good because I had a toothache. Where's a good place to get your teeth checked?

Tim:　There's a good dentist on Maple Street. I'll email you the address.

Sally:　Thanks, Tim. How about going for lunch tomorrow?

Tim:　I'm sorry, Sally. I'm really busy tomorrow — maybe some other time.

提姆：嗨，莎莉。妳有沒有聽說我們今年有紅利可以拿？

莎莉：好極了。你知不知道會有多少？

提姆：並不知道。嘿，妳的週末過得如何？

莎莉：不怎麼樣，因為我牙痛。有什麼好地方可以檢查牙齒？

提姆：楓葉街上有一個牙醫不錯。我會把地址用電子郵件寄給妳。

莎莉：謝了，提姆。明天一起去吃個午飯如何？

提姆：對不起，莎莉，我明天很忙，也許下一次吧。

Chapter **5** 保持談話熱度與結束談話

Ｉ 1. (C) 2. (A) 3. (C)

ＩＩ 1. (B) 2. (A)

❶ 很高興又見到你。

(A) 謝謝。

(B) 我也很高興見到你。

(C) 不客氣。

❷ 你現在在忙嗎？

(A) 是的，對不起。

(B) 不用，謝謝。

(C) 是的，我最近滿忙的。

ＩＩＩ 範例解答

Shelly: Hi Dan. Is now a good time to talk?
Dan:　　Sure.
Shelly: Did you get my email?
Dan:　　No, I didn't.
Shelly: Really? Are you sure?
Dan:　　Yes. When did you send it?
Shelly: I can't remember. It was about a job opportunity.
Dan:　　Really? Tell me more.
Shelly: Sorry, I've got to go. I'll send you another.

榭莉　：嗨，丹。現在方便說話嗎？
丹　　：方便。
榭莉　：你有沒有收到我的電子郵件？
丹　　：沒有，沒收到。
榭莉　：真的嗎？你確定嗎？
丹　　：確定。妳什麼時候寄的？
榭莉　：我不記得了。那封信是關於一個工作機會。
丹　　：真的嗎？多告訴我一些。
榭莉　：抱歉，我得走了。我會再寄另一封給你。

Chapter
6 請求協助與回應他人請求

I 1. (B) 2. (B) 3. (B)

II 1. (C) 2. (A)

❶ 我在想，不知道可不可以借用你的車？
    (A) 多謝了。
    (B) 因為我明天需要用它。
    (C) 對不起，不行。
❷ 拿去吧。
    (A) 我真的很感激。
    (B) 還是謝謝你。
    (C) 去上班。

III 範例解答

Linda: Hi Dennis. I was wondering if I could use your camera?
Dennis: Sure, no problem. Here you go.
Linda: Thanks. I really appreciate it. Also, would you mind lending me your notebook on Friday morning?
Dennis: I don't think so. I need it on Friday morning. Sorry.

琳達　 ：嗨，丹尼斯。我在想，不知道可不可以借用你的相機？
丹尼斯：當然，沒問題。拿去吧。
琳達　 ：謝謝。我真的很感激。還有，你介不介意星期五早上把筆記型電腦借給我？
丹尼斯：我想不行。我星期五早上需要用它。抱歉。

Chapter 7 評論好消息與壞消息

I 1. (B) 2. (C) 3. (C)

II 1. (C) 2. (B)

❶ 幹得好。

   (A) 到我家。

   (B) 我很好，謝謝。

   (C) 謝謝。

❷ 我剛被開除了！

   (A) 恭喜！

   (B) 你還好嗎？

   (C) 覆水難收。

III 範例解答

Dean: I got a new job today.
Lori:　That's great. Way to go!
Dean: Thanks, but I also have some bad news. I lost my wallet.
Lori:　What a shame. I'm sorry to hear that. How is your wife these days?
Dean: We're getting a divorce.
Lori:　Please forgive me — I didn't know.
Dean: That's OK. I'm feeling pretty bad about it right now.
Lori:　Well, tomorrow's another day. I hope you feel better then.

狄恩：我今天找到了一份新工作。
蘿莉：太好了。做得好！
狄恩：謝謝，不過我也有些壞消息。我的皮夾弄丟了。
蘿莉：真令人遺憾。很遺憾聽你這麼說。你太太最近如何？
狄恩：我們在辦離婚。
蘿莉：請原諒我，我並不知道。
狄恩：沒關係。我現在覺得挺難過的。
蘿莉：嗯，明天又是全新的一天，希望你到時會感覺好一些。

Chapter 8 商務電話用語

I 1. (C) 2. (A) 3. (B)

II 1. (A) 2. (B)

❶ 請問是哪位？

   (A) 我是史蒂芬。

   (B) 我，史蒂芬。

   (C) 我就是。

❷ 對不起，電話忙線中。

   (A) 我幫你轉接。

   (B) 沒關係，我等。

   (C) 不，我現在不忙。

III 範例解答

Stan: Good afternoon. May I speak to Candy please?

Stephanie: May I ask who's calling, please?

Stan: This is Stan.

Stephanie: I'll put you through. Oh, I'm sorry. The line is busy. Would you like to leave a message?

Stan: Yes, thanks. Please ask her to call me.

史丹：   午安。能不能麻煩請甘蒂接電話？

史蒂芬妮： 請問您是哪位？

史丹：   我是史丹。

史蒂芬妮： 我幫您轉過去。噢，對不起，電話忙線中。您要不要留言？

史丹：   好，謝謝。麻煩請她再打給我。

Chapter
9 談論器材設備問題

I 1. (B) 2. (A) 3. (C)

II 1. (A) 2. (C)

❶ 我們的紙用完了。

(A) 我再去拿一些。

(B) 去哪裡？

(C) 它毀了。

❷ 印表機報銷了。

(A) 你能教我如何使用它嗎？

(B) 我對它不太了解。

(C) 我們應該把它換掉。

III 範例解答

Daisy: Jerry, something is wrong with the printer. I think it needs fixing.

Jerry: Are you sure it's broken?

Daisy: No, I'm not sure. Maybe I'm doing something wrong. Could you show me how to use it?

Jerry: Sure, I hope it's not wrecked. Oh, here's your problem — the printer has just run out of paper.

黛西： 傑瑞，印表機有些不太對勁。我想它需要修理。

傑瑞： 妳確定它故障了嗎？

黛西： 不，我不確定，也許我弄錯了什麼。你能教我如何使用它嗎？

傑瑞： 當然，我希望它不是壞了。噢，問題在這裡，印表機的紙用完了。

Chapter
10　處理溝通障礙

I　1. (C)　2. (A)　3. (B)

II　1. (C)　2. (A)

❶ 我不懂你的意思。

　(A) 我一頭霧水。

　(B) 你要去哪裡？

　(C) 讓我重說一遍。

❷ 我沒聽清楚。

　(A) 讓我再重說一遍。

　(B) 我也是。

　(C) 拿去吧。

III 範例解答

Vicki:　I'm sorry, Ted. I don't follow you.

Ted:　I said the document must be notarized. Do you know what I mean?

Vicki:　No. What did you mean by "notarized?"

Ted:　You know, something that is witnessed by a notary public.

Vicki:　I'm lost. What is a notary public?

Ted:　It's a person with a special licence who can legally witness the signing of documents.

Vicki:　I see.

維琪：　抱歉，泰德，我不懂你的意思。

泰德：　我說那份文件必須經過公證。妳知道我是什麼意思嗎？

維琪：　不知道。你說「公證」是什麼意思？

泰德：　妳知道嘛，就是某樣東西要經過公證人見證。

維琪：　我一頭霧水。什麼叫公證人？

泰德：　就是一個有特殊的執照的人，可以合法見證文件簽署。

維琪：　我懂了。

notarize [ˋnotəˏræz] v.（公證人）證明（文件）

notary [ˋnotərɪ] n. 公證人 (= notary public)

witness [ˋwɪtnɪs] v.（在……簽名）作證

Chapter 11 處理批評

I 1. (B) 2. (B) 3. (C)

II 1. (B) 2. (C)

❶ 這是誰做的？

(A) 是你的責任。

(B) 是我的錯。

(C) 這是無法接受的。

❷ 是你的錯。

(A) 這是怎麼發生的？

(B) 該怪誰？

(C) 不會再發生了。

III 範例解答

Gloria: Vince, how did this happen?

Vince: Sorry, Gloria, I'm to blame.

Gloria: It was your responsibility to make sure the contract was right. It's your fault we lost the deal. That's unacceptable.

Vince: I'm very sorry. I won't repeat the same mistake.

葛蘿莉亞： 文斯，這是怎麼發生的？

文斯： 抱歉，葛蘿莉亞，應該怪我。

葛蘿莉亞： 確定合約無誤是你的責任。我們失去這筆生意是你的錯。這是無法接受的。

文斯： 非常對不起，我不會再犯同樣的錯。

Chapter
12 道歉與解釋

Ⅰ 1. (A) 2. (B) 3. (B)

Ⅱ 1. (A) 2. (C)

❶ 那是個意外。

(A) 沒關係。

(B) 意外在哪裡？

(C) 我非常抱歉。

❷ 弄壞你的相機我覺得很過意不去。

(A) 你應該吃一些藥。

(B) 你去看醫生了嗎？

(C) 別放在心上。

Ⅲ 範例解答

Fran: Bill, I apologize for spilling my coffee on you. Please forgive me. I didn't mean to.

Bill:　That's OK, Fran.

Fran: It's because I'm really tired today. The reason is I didn't sleep well last night.

Bill:　You should get more sleep.

Fran: I drank a lot of coffee last night; therefore I couldn't get to sleep.

法蘭：比爾，對不起我把咖啡灑在你身上。請原諒我，我不是故意的。

比爾：沒關係，法蘭。

法蘭：因為我今天真的很累，原因是我昨晚沒睡好。

比爾：妳應該多睡一下。

法蘭：我昨晚喝了很多咖啡，因此睡不著。

Chapter 13 談論職場事務

I 1. (B) 2. (C) 3. (B)

II 1. (A) 2. (B)

❶ 生意正蓬勃發展。

(A) 太好了。

(B) 真慘。

(C) 小心。

❷ 我的公司破產了。

(A) 那很好。

(B) 我很遺憾聽你這麼說。

(C) 在銀行做事很不錯。

III 範例解答

Oliver: Hi May. How is your new job?

May: Pretty good. The pay is not bad, but I have to work overtime a lot. What about you?

Oliver: I just got hired by a computer company. They make very small computers and there's a demand for that kind of product now.

May: I know. That market is really hot at the moment. But why did you change jobs?

Oliver: My old company went out of business.

奧利佛：嗨，梅，妳的新工作如何？

梅：　　很不錯。薪水還不差，但是我常常得加班。你呢？

奧利佛：我剛被一家電腦公司錄用。他們生產非常小型的電腦，而現在這種產品有其需求。

梅：　　我知道，那個市場現在真的很熱。不過你為什麼換工作？

奧利佛：我以前的公司倒閉了。

Chapter

14 讓上司印象深刻與讚美同事

I 1. (C)　2. (B)　3. (C)

II 1. (C)　2. (A)

❶ 我會確保自己會有好的表現。

　　(A) 不，我不確定。

　　(B) 是的，這是好的表現。

　　(C) 那很好。

❷ 我很感激。

　　(A) 不客氣。

　　(B) 做得好。

　　(C) 你太客氣了。

III 範例解答

Amanda: Eric, I give you my word this report will not be late. You can count on me.

Eric:　　Thanks, Amanda. I'm impressed with your confidence.

Amanda: I'll ensure I give it to you by 5 p.m. on Friday — I promise.

Eric:　　Good. By the way, you look good today, Amanda.

Amanda: Thanks.

艾曼達：　艾瑞克，我向你承諾這份報告絕不會延遲。你可以依賴我。

艾瑞克：　謝謝，艾曼達。我對妳的信心印象非常深刻。

艾曼達：　我會確保我在星期五下午五點前把它交給你，我保證。

艾瑞克：　好。對了，妳今天看起來很不錯，艾曼達。

艾曼達：　謝謝。

Chapter

15 辦公室八卦

I 1. (B) 2. (C) 3. (A)

II 1. (B) 2. (C)

❶ 你想知道一個秘密嗎？

(A) 我什麼秘密都不知道。

(B) 好啊，當然。

(C) 我真不敢相信。

❷ 不可能！

(A) 是的，這是真的。

(B) 對不起。

(C) 你從哪裡聽來的？

III 範例解答

Melinda: Hi Nick. What's up?

Nick: Well, I heard from someone that there will be some layoffs.

Melinda: I can't believe it! Who told you? Is that for certain?

Nick: I heard it from my boss. Actually, it doesn't surprise me — the company has been losing money for years.

瑪琳達： 嗨，尼克。有什麼消息？

尼克： 嗯，我聽某人說會有幾個人被裁員。

瑪琳達： 我真不敢相信！是誰告訴你的？此事確定嗎？

尼克： 我是聽我上司說的。事實上，我並不驚訝，公司已經連續好幾年都虧錢了。

Chapter 16　談論目標與未來計畫

I　1. (C)　2. (B)　3. (B)

II　1. (B)　2. (B)

❶ 我有個夢想希望能成為醫生。

(A) 我睡的很好。

(B) 聽起來很棒。

(C) 做得不錯。

❷ 你未來的計畫是什麼？

(A) 我明天要去看牙醫。

(B) 我要成為一名牙醫。

(C) 我的成就包括成為一名牙醫。

III 範例解答

Ernie:　Penny, what are your future goals?

Penny:　I'm going to go to graduate school. What about you? Where do you want to be in a few years?

Ernie:　My goal is to start my own company. I hope to have a computer company someday.

Penny:　That sounds great. Good luck.

爾尼：　潘妮，妳未來的目標是什麼？

潘妮：　我要去念研究所。你呢？你在幾年後想要達成什麼目標？

爾尼：　我的目標是創設自己的公司。我希望有一天可以擁有一家電腦公司。

潘妮：　聽起來很棒。祝你好運。

國家圖書館出版品預行編目資料

搞定辦公室英文 = Office English ／ Brian Foden
作；何岱耘譯. ――初版. ――臺北市：貝塔,
2006〔民95〕　面：　　公分
　　ISBN 957-729-584-3（平裝）
　　1. 商業英語―會話
805.188　　　　　　　　　　　　95005132

搞定辦公室英文
Office English

作　　者／Brian Foden
總 編 審／王復國
譯　　者／何岱耘
執行編輯／莊碧娟

出　　版／貝塔出版有限公司
地　　址／100 台北市館前路 12 號 11 樓
電　　話／(02)2314-2525
傳　　真／(02)2312-3535
郵　　撥／19493777 貝塔出版有限公司
客服專線／(02)2314-3535
客服信箱／btservice@betamedia.com.tw

總 經 銷／時報文化出版企業股份有限公司
地　　址／桃園縣龜山鄉萬壽路二段 351 號
電　　話／(02) 2306-6842

出版日期／2006 年 5 月初版一刷
定　　價／320 元
ISBN：957-729-584-3

喚醒你的英文語感！

対折後釘好，直接寄回即可！

100 台北市中正區館前路12號11樓

 貝塔語言出版 收
Beta Multimedia Publishing

寄件者住址 ☐☐☐ _____

_____

謝謝您購買本書！！

貝塔語言擁有最優良之英文學習書籍，為提供您最佳的英語學習資訊，您可填妥此表後寄回（免貼郵票）將可不定期收到本公司最新發行書訊及活動訊息！

姓名：＿＿＿＿＿＿＿＿＿＿＿＿　性別：□男 □女　生日：＿＿＿年＿＿＿月＿＿＿日

電話：(公)＿＿＿＿＿＿＿＿＿＿(宅)＿＿＿＿＿＿＿＿＿＿(手機)＿＿＿＿＿＿＿＿＿＿

電子信箱：＿＿＿＿＿＿＿＿＿＿＿＿＿＿＿＿＿＿＿＿＿＿＿＿＿＿

學歷：□高中職含以下　□專科　□大學　□研究所含以上

職業：□金融　□服務　□傳播　□製造　□資訊　□軍公教　□出版
　　　□自由　□教育　□學生　□其他

職級：□企業負責人　□高階主管　□中階主管　□職員　□專業人士

1. 您購買的書籍是？＿＿＿＿＿＿＿＿＿＿＿＿＿＿＿＿＿＿＿＿

2. 您從何處得知本產品？(可複選)
　　　□書店 □網路 □書展 □校園活動 □廣告信函 □他人推薦 □新聞報導 □其他

3. 您覺得本產品價格：
　　　□偏高 □合理 □偏低

4. 請問目前您每週花了多少時間學英語？
　　　□ 不到十分鐘 □ 十分鐘以上，但不到半小時 □ 半小時以上，但不到一小時
　　　□ 一小時以上，但不到兩小時 □ 兩個小時以上 □ 不一定

5. 通常在選擇語言學習書時，哪些因素是您會考慮的？
　　　□ 封面 □ 內容、實用性 □ 品牌 □ 媒體、朋友推薦 □ 價格□ 其他＿＿＿＿＿＿

6. 市面上您最需要的語言書種類為？
　　　□ 聽力 □ 閱讀 □ 文法 □ 口說 □ 寫作 □ 其他＿＿＿＿＿＿

7. 通常您會透過何種方式選購語言學習書籍？
　　　□ 書店門市 □ 網路書店 □ 郵購 □ 直接找出版社 □ 學校或公司團購
　　　□ 其他＿＿＿＿＿＿＿

8. 給我們的建議：＿＿＿＿＿＿＿＿＿＿＿＿＿＿＿＿＿＿＿＿＿＿＿
＿＿＿＿＿＿＿＿＿＿＿＿＿＿＿＿＿＿＿＿＿＿＿＿＿＿＿＿＿＿

唤醒你的英文語感！

Get a Feel for English !

喚醒你的英文語感！

Get a Feel for English !